Praise for KJ Charles's
Think of England

"A wonderfully entertaining, old-school amateur-spy mystery and a delicious opposites-attract romance in one...a fully satisfying, funny and entertaining reading experience."
~ *Prism Book Alliance*

"I have totally fallen in love with Curtis and Daniel and was thrilled to hear Charles plans more for them. Excellent story and very highly recommended."
~ *Joyfully Jay*

"By giving us complex and wounded characters, thrilling suspense, a powerful threat, and high emotional stakes, Ms. Charles has crafted a compelling story that I couldn't put down."
~ *Fresh Fiction*

"*Downton Abbey* meets M/M romance—an absolutely brilliant historical novel with industrial espionage, murder, blackmail and two unlikely heroes up against the odds."
~ *Sinfully Sexy Book Reviews*

"That bad-guy, evil plan stuff is fun, but I mostly enjoyed watching two men who are so obviously wrong for each other and have nothing in common turn out to be a swoon-worthy perfect match."
~ *Heroes and Heartbreakers*

Look for these titles by
KJ Charles

Now Available:

Non-Stop Till Tokyo
Think of England

A Charm of Magpies
The Magpie Lord
A Case of Possession
A Case of Spirits
Flight of Magpies
Jackdaw

Think of England

KJ Charles

Samhain Publishing, Ltd.
11821 Mason Montgomery Road, 4B
Cincinnati, OH 45249
www.samhainpublishing.com

Think of England
Copyright © 2014 by KJ Charles
Print ISBN: 978-1-61922-614-2
Digital ISBN: 978-1-61922-177-2

Editing by Anne Scott
Cover by Erin Dameron-Hill

First Samhain Publishing, Ltd. electronic publication: July 2014
First Samhain Publishing, Ltd. print publication: July 2015

Dedication

For Natalie, who is brilliant.

Acknowledgments

Sir Henry Curtis and the Kukuana Place of Death are the creations of H. Rider Haggard in his classic 1885 romp *King Solomon's Mines*. Archie is my unauthorised addition to the Curtis family tree. I felt it could take the shake-up.

With thanks to the TFR goons (for gun advice) and Alexandra Sherriff (for *very serious* psychology input).

Chapter One

October 1904

The train up from London took hours, a weary ride for a man who was too tense to sleep and too busy with his thoughts to read. He would have preferred to motor, but that was impossible now.

There was a car waiting at the station, the latest model Austin. The uniformed chauffeur stood by it with military bearing, but leapt to help as Curtis approached and hovered while he got himself into the passenger seat, solicitously offering blankets against the evening chill in the autumnal air. He waved them away.

"Are you sure, sir? Lady Armstrong gave instructions—"

"I'm not an invalid."

"No, Captain Curtis." The chauffeur touched his cap in salute.

"I'm not an officer either."

"I beg your pardon, sir."

It was a long drive to Peakholme. They avoided the industrial areas of Newcastle, though he saw the black smoke thick against the darkened skies. It was only a few miles before they had left the city quite behind and were driving through the open country. Farmland turned to scrub and rose into the foothills of the Pennines, and at last they headed up an otherwise empty winding road onto a bleak and open hillside.

"Is it much further?" he asked.

"Nearly there, sir," the chauffeur assured him. "See that spot of light ahead?"

Curtis blinked against the cold, but he did see light on the hillside, and soon made out a darker shape round it. "It's a touch bare round here for a country house," he remarked.

"Yes, sir. Sir Hubert always says, it's bare now, but just you come back in a hundred years." The chauffeur chuckled loyally. Curtis made a mental wager with himself how many times Sir Hubert would come out with that witticism during his stay.

The Austin purred through the recent plantations which would, in that much-anticipated century, become a magnificent forest surrounding Peakholme. At long last they pulled up outside the great new house, bright yellow light spilling from the doorway. A servant was waiting on the drive to open the car door. Curtis bit back the grunt of pain as his knee straightened. He flexed his leg a couple of times before crunching over the gravel to the stone steps where a footman waited to take his coat.

"Mr. Curtis!" cried Lady Armstrong, coming into the brightly lit hall to greet him. Her dress was a marvellous confection in blue, frothing around her bare shoulders and setting off her fair hair to perfection. She would have looked dashing in London, let alone this remote region. "How wonderful to have you here. It's such a pilgrimage to reach us, isn't it? I'm so happy you could come." She held out both hands for his, her characteristic, charmingly informal greeting. He gave her his left hand, withholding the right, and saw a flash of concern or pity on her face, stifled almost at once. "Thank you so much for joining our little party. Hubert!"

"Here, my dear." Sir Hubert had come into the corridor behind her. He was a stout, bald-headed man, a good three decades older than his wife, with a benevolent look that was at odds with his professional reputation. "Well, well, Archie Curtis." They performed a pantomime handshake, Sir Hubert's hand surrounding Curtis's but barely touching it. "It's a great pleasure to see you. How's that uncle of yours?"

"In Africa, sir."

"Good heavens, again? He always had itchy feet, Henry did. When we were at school he was forever breaking bounds, you know. I should be delighted to see the old chap some time, and that naval pal of his. I suppose they're still jaunting around together?"

"As usual, sir." Sir Henry Curtis had been left with the care of his youngest brother's orphaned child when Archie was just two months old. Sir Henry and his inseparable friend and neighbour Captain Good had raised the boy between them, for years curtailing their trips to far-flung regions so that they were there each summer when he returned from school. He had grown up assuming that easy, uncomplicated companionship was the natural order of things. Now, it seemed a lost Eden.

"Well, I trust we'll give you a good enough time that you'll encourage them to visit. And how are you, my dear fellow? I was so very sorry to hear about your injury." That was no platitude, Sir Hubert's eyes were full of concern. "That was a bad business, a dreadful mistake. It shouldn't have happened to you."

Lady Armstrong broke in with a rippling laugh. "My dear, Mr. Curtis has had a terribly long journey. We'll be dining in an hour. Wesley will take you up. The east corridor, Wesley," she told a well-built servant in Peakholme's dark green livery.

Curtis followed the man up the wide stairs, leaning a little on the banister rail and admiring the house as he went. Sir Hubert, a wealthy industrialist, had had Peakholme built to his own specification some fifteen years ago. It had been an extraordinarily modern creation at that time, equipped with the very latest innovations, with running water in all the bathrooms, heated by hot-water radiators and illuminated throughout by electricity from his own hydroelectric generator.

These luxuries were becoming quite familiar in London hotels, but to find them in such measure in a private house so far from the centre of things was still a surprise.

The long hallways on which the electric lamps shed their bright yellow light, reliable and clean but so much more glaring than gaslight, seemed conventional enough otherwise. Sir Hubert's son was well known to be hunting mad, and it seemed to be a family trait, since the passageways were hung with oils of fox-chasing scenes and lined with stuffed birds of prey in glass cases, all in dramatic poses. An owl stooped, wings sharply bent, in the act of catching a mouse; a hawk leaned off a branch, ready to launch into the attack; an eagle glared with glassy eyes. Curtis registered them as landmarks in a house that wasn't altogether easy to negotiate.

"This is a rather unusual arrangement," he remarked to the servant.

"Yes, sir," Wesley agreed. "The house is laid out to permit a service corridor running behind the bedrooms here. That's to allow for the electrical wiring, and the centralised heating." He spoke the technical words with pride. "Marvellous thing, the electrical. I don't know if you're familiar with its operation, sir?" he asked hopefully, opening the door to a room at the end of the corridor.

"Please, demonstrate." Curtis, a practical man, was quite familiar with electricity, but this tour was obviously the highlight of the servant's day, so he let Wesley show him the miracles of buttons that summoned servants, and switches that brought illumination or operated an overhead fan. Given the chill in the outside air this cold October, let alone the house's position in the north of England, he doubted he would require the latter.

There was a large gilt-framed mirror on the inner wall of the room, opposite the bed. Curtis glanced at himself, assessing his travel-stained state, and caught Wesley's eye in the glass.

"Welcome to Peakholme, sir, if I may be so bold." The servant was watching his reflected face, without dropping his eyes. "If there's anything I can do for you during your stay, sir, please ring. You don't have a man, I believe?"

"No." Curtis turned from the mirror.

"Then may I assist you now, sir?"

"No. Thank you. Unpack for me later, please. Otherwise I'll ring if I need you."

"I hope you will, sir." Wesley accepted the shilling Curtis gave him, but hesitated a moment. "If there's anything else...?"

Curtis wondered what the man was hanging around for; the tip had been generous enough. "That'll be all."

"Yes, Mr. Curtis."

Wesley left the room, and Curtis sat heavily on the bed, giving himself a moment before he had to change and get ready to face his fellow guests.

He didn't know if he could do this. What was he playing at, coming here? What did he think he could achieve?

He had used to enjoy house parties, in the days when they were rare oases of entertainment and relaxation between military postings. He had attended three since he had retired from the war a year and a half ago, jollied along by all the people who told him that he had to come out of his shell, rejoin society, be a good fellow. Each visit had felt more arid than the last, its activity more pointless, the frenetic self-indulgence of people whose lives held nothing but the pursuit of pleasure.

At least he was at this party with some sort of purpose, even if, now, his purpose seemed so unlikely as to be absurd.

He stripped the black leather glove off his right hand and flexed his thumb and forefinger. The scar tissue that covered his knuckles, where the other fingers used to be, was tight. He rubbed it with the softening ointment for a few minutes, thinking about the work ahead, then pulled the disguising glove back over the gnarled mess of mutilated flesh and began to dress for dinner.

It wasn't too much of a chore, although perhaps he should have let the man Wesley remain. But he'd had eighteen months to get used to managing studs and buttons with fewer fingers, and to preserve his independence in dress only took him perhaps three times as long as when he had been an able-bodied man.

He adjusted his white piqué waistcoat and tweaked the collar points to his satisfaction. A little pomade controlled his thick blond hair's tendency to wave, and he was ready.

He assessed himself in the mirror. He was dressed like a gentleman; with his bearing and his skin tanned by the African sun, he still had the air of a soldier. He didn't look like a spy, a sneak, a liar. And, unfortunately, he didn't feel much like one either.

He was the last into the drawing room, and Lady Armstrong clapped her hands for attention. "My dears, our final guest. Mr. Archie Curtis. Sir Henry Curtis's nephew, you know, the explorer." There was a murmur. Curtis smiled, resigned to this by a lifetime of similar introductions. The adventurous African trip that had made his uncle rich some twenty-five years ago was still a matter of public fascination.

"And now, I must introduce you to everyone," Lady Armstrong went on. "Miss Carruth and Miss Merton." Miss Carruth was a pretty, vital young woman in her early twenties, dashingly dressed and with a twinkle in her pansy-brown eyes. Miss Merton, who seemed to be her companion, was a couple of years older with a plainer style and a watchful look, but she murmured the right courtesies.

"Mr. Keston Grayling and Mrs. Grayling, of Hull." Provincial money, Curtis thought, as the couple smiled their greetings. Mr.

Grayling looked a rather silly sort of chap, expensively dressed but lacking polish, and with a hint of double chin. Mrs. Grayling wore a gown that was cut rather too tight and too low for Curtis's approval. He wondered if she was the sort of lady who enjoyed a little country-house intrigue, of the conventional kind.

"My brother John Lambdon, and Mrs. Lambdon." In this pair it was the man who looked like he passed between bedrooms. Lambdon had his sister's striking good looks and was well-built enough, though not of Curtis's breadth. Mrs. Lambdon was a pallid presence beside him, with lank hair, a limp hand, and the air of the professional headache-sufferer.

"Hubert's son, James." Curtis knew this was the product of Sir Hubert's first marriage. The man looked to be in his late twenties, no more than five years younger than the current Lady Armstrong. He had a cheerful look on a broad, open face, which was weathered by outdoor pursuits and bore no great signs of intelligence.

"Curtis, good to meet you." James Armstrong put his hand out. Curtis extended his own right hand and winced as the young man took it, his powerful grip crushing the scar tissue.

"Darling, I did tell you," said Lady Armstrong, voice sharp.

"Oh, so sorry, mater." Armstrong gave her an apologetic smile, then turned it to Curtis. "Completely slipped my mind, what."

"Mr. Peter Holt. James's dear friend," Lady Armstrong went on. The man she indicated was a striking piece of work. He matched Curtis's own size and build, a good six foot two, with powerful shoulders, a nose that had been broken at least once, and a pugilistic air. His bright, observant hazel eyes suggested intelligence as well as strength, and his grip on Curtis's hand was definite, without painful pressure. A man who knew how to use his muscles.

Impressive, Curtis thought, then frowned in an effort at memory. "Were you at Oxford?"

Holt smiled, pleased to be recognised. "Keble. A couple of years below you."

"Mr. Holt took a boxing blue as well," Lady Armstrong put in.

"Of course. I'll have seen you in...Fenton's?"

"On Broad Street, yes. I wasn't in your league, though," Holt said with cheerful frankness. "I was at your fight with Gilliam. Superb match."

Curtis grinned reminiscently. "Hardest fight of my life."

"You two may talk boxing all you like when I've completed the introductions," Lady Armstrong put in. "Mr. Curtis, this is Mr. da Silva."

Curtis looked at the gentleman indicated and decided on the spot that he'd rarely seen a more dislikable man.

He was about Curtis's age and just a few inches shorter, close to six foot, but with nothing of his own bulk. A slender, willowy sort, and very dark, with sleek and glossy black hair, brilliantined to within an inch of its life, and eyes of such a deep shade that it was nearly impossible to tell pupil from iris. His skin was olive-tinted against his white shirt. In fact, he was quite obviously some kind of foreigner.

A foreigner and a dandy, because while his shirt was impeccable and the tailcoat and tapering trousers cut to perfection, he was wearing a huge green glass ring and, Curtis saw with dawning horror, a bright green flower in his buttonhole.

Da Silva walked a few steps over, giving Curtis just enough time to register that he affected a sinuous sort of movement, and offered him a hand so limp that he struggled not to drop it like a dead animal.

"Charmed," drawled da Silva. Somewhat to Curtis's surprise, his accent was that of an Englishman of breeding. "A military gentleman and a pugilist, how delightful. I do enjoy spending time with our brave boys." He gave Curtis a curling smile and moved away, snake-hipped, taking Lady Armstrong with him as the party formed little groups.

"Well. Who's that chap?" asked Curtis quietly.

"Dreadful dago," said James, not quietly. "I've no idea why Sophie tolerates the man."

"Oh, he's terribly amusing, and so clever." The pretty Miss Carruth smiled at Curtis. "I'm Fenella Carruth, in case you didn't catch all those names. How do you know the Armstrongs? Through your uncle? He sounds like a wonderful man."

They made small talk about that and Miss Carruth's industrialist father, who had designed Peakholme's telephone exchange, before they were called in to dinner. Curtis found himself seated between Miss Carruth and the drab Mrs. Lambdon, with his fellow Oxford man Holt on Miss Carruth's other side. The younger lady was sparkling with witty repartee, daring without ever going beyond the bounds, and Holt returned some dashingly flirtatious comments. He was making his interest in Miss Carruth clear; her responses were flattering enough but neatly brought in both Curtis and James Armstrong, seated opposite, inviting them to compete for her attention. It seemed she liked to have a following of suitors.

Curtis couldn't bring himself to play along. He could imagine his Uncle Maurice's groaning despair at his lack of enthusiasm: Miss Carruth was a pretty, pleasant and wealthy young woman, just the sort he ought to be looking for, now he had no reason not to settle down. But he felt no desire to cut the other two men out and couldn't have done it if he'd wanted to, since he had never been gifted at flirtation or banter and had no idea how people came up with quick, clever remarks and retorts. He managed a couple of appropriate responses, for the sake of appearances, but his concentration was on the tiresome demands of manipulating cutlery with his damaged hand, and on watching the company.

They seemed a normal country-house set. The Graylings and Lambdons looked to be unremarkable couples; the two single ladies were very pleasant. James Armstrong and Peter Holt were typical young men about town, James with more money, Holt with more brains. Da Silva stood out from the company as one of the "Bloomsbury" sort popping up in society like mushrooms, effete, artistic, disconcertingly modern to a solid Victorian soul like Curtis. It was quite clear why Lady Armstrong had invited the fellow, though. He had an astonishingly quick tongue, and his witty, waspish remarks set the whole company laughing on several occasions throughout the meal. Curtis didn't find him any more likeable for it—he had spent three years at Oxford avoiding those poisonous decadent types, with their vicious remarks and knowing smiles—but all the same, he had to admit the fellow was amusing. Only Holt's chuckles seemed rather perfunctory. Maybe he was concerned that da Silva would outshine his own conversation in front of Miss Carruth. Curtis didn't think he needed to worry about a rival there.

There was nobody of Sir Hubert's age present: his wife filled the house with guests of her own generation. Perhaps her husband felt younger for the company. It was hard to tell, since he made few remarks, but he beamed pleasantly enough on his guests, and the conversation flowed without difficulty until the ladies departed the table and their host called for port.

"I say, Curtis," Grayling said, passing the decanter. "Do I understand you were in the war?"

"I was."

"Injured?" Lambdon gestured at his hand.

Curtis nodded. "At Jacobsdal."

"What was that, a battle?" asked Grayling. He was a little the worse for wine and trying to disguise it by attempting intelligent questions.

"No. Not a battle." Curtis poured himself a glass of port, gripping the neck of the decanter with his finger and thumb, his left hand under it to support its weight.

"No, that's right, it was the sabotage business, wasn't it?"

"That was never proved." Sir Hubert's tone was intended to quell that line of conversation.

Curtis ignored the hint. He hated talking about this subject, hated thinking about it, but this was what he was here for, and there might not be another opportunity, not with Sir Hubert so evidently unwilling to discuss it. "My company was at Jacobsdal waiting for reinforcements when we got a shipment of supplies. Much needed."

"The supply lines in the war were dreadful," said Lambdon, with all the authority of a man who'd read newspapers.

"We were hoping for boots, we got a few crates of guns. A new sort. Lafayette manufacture. They were welcome enough, of course. We had a few days in hand and any amount of ammunition supplied, so we thought we'd best get used to them. We shared them amongst ourselves and spread out to give them a try."

He stopped there, taking a gulp of port to disguise the sudden tightening of his throat, because even all these months on, the words brought back the smell. The scent of Africa's hot dry earth, and the cordite, and the blood.

"And the guns were faulty." Sir Hubert clearly wanted this story over with.

"Not the word, sir. They burst in our hands. Exploding all over the field." Curtis lifted his gloved right hand, just slightly. "I lost three fingers when the stock of my revolver blew. The man next to me—" Lieutenant Fisher, that warm, laughing redheaded Scot who had been his tentmate for two years, falling

19

to his knees, mouth open in bewilderment as blood poured from the shattered mess of his wrist. Dying, there on the field, as Curtis tried to reach him, holding out the bloody ruin of his own hand for a touch that would never happen.

He couldn't speak of that. "It was a damned business. My company lost as many men in two minutes' practice firing as in six months of war before it." Seven deaths on the field; six more in the field hospital; two suicides, later. Three men blinded. Mutilations and amputations. "The entire crate of guns was deadly."

"*Inappropriately* deadly," da Silva murmured.

Lambdon asked, "Was anything ever proved against the Lafayette company, Hubert?"

"The inquiry was inconclusive." Sir Hubert's face had been serious throughout Curtis's recital, hearing the story with distaste, but nothing more. "The manufacturing process was at fault, of course, the walls of the chambers were catastrophically weak, but nobody found it to be anything but an accident. *I* never believed it was anything else. Lafayette was mad for economy, all of us in the trade knew that. Always finding ways to squeeze an extra penny from a pound. There needs be no more to it than that he cut one corner too many."

James Armstrong put on a knowing look. "But you didn't like his politics, did you, pater? I thought you said he didn't support the war."

Sir Hubert gave his son a frown. "Nothing was ever found against him, and the man's dead."

"Dead? What happened to him?" Grayling asked.

"He was found floating in the Thames, a couple of weeks ago," said Sir Hubert heavily. "He must have slipped and fallen in."

James made a sceptical noise. "We all know what that means. Guilt, if you ask me."

Sir Hubert frowned. "Enough of this. John, were you at Goodwood for the last race?"

Lambdon's answer turned the talk to sport, and most of the company were soon exchanging remarks on their preferred activities. Curtis and Holt had a fair few boxing acquaintances in common, and the familiar talk relaxed him, driving the more recent memories away. The others discussed shooting and cricket. Da Silva did not join in the conversation, but sat with a faint, abstracted smile that radiated polite boredom, and sipped the excellent port with the air of a man who would have preferred absinthe.

What a bloody pansy, Curtis thought.

It was a perfectly standard social evening, but in no way a fruitful one, and as he worked the studs out of his collar that night, Curtis had to admit to his reflection that he had no great idea how to change that.

Chapter Two

The next morning was a bright blue October day, the sun spilling yellow over the surrounding hills and peaks, and Lady Armstrong had plans for her guests.

"A march over the hills, to be followed by a picnic lunch, my dears." She clapped her hands. "Blow away those cobwebs. We have plenty of walking things in all sizes." She dragooned the company irresistibly, until she came up against two immovable objects.

Curtis was the first. "It sounds marvellous, but I can't chance it. I took a bullet in the knee at Jacobsdal." A stray round from a panicking colleague, tearing through his leg even as he stared at his ruined hand. "It's much better these days but rough terrain is tricky, and train journeys play hob with it. I should rest it today if I'm to be up for the rest of the week."

"Oh, but we can order the carriage—or a horse?"

"There's no need to take the trouble. I've plenty of reading to catch up on." Curtis spoke as firmly as he could, hoping she wouldn't argue.

"I shall keep Mr. Curtis company," came a silky voice over his shoulder.

Curtis repressed a grimace. Lady Armstrong frowned. "Now, really, Mr. da Silva, you must have some fresh air and exercise."

"My dear lady, my constitution would scarcely survive such a thing. Simply *inhaling* in the countryside is as much exertion as I can bear. All that healthful freshness, so bad for the soul." Da Silva shuddered dramatically. Miss Carruth giggled. "No; I shall apply myself to my labours. I must toil."

"At what?" Curtis felt compelled to ask.

"The poetical art." Da Silva was resplendent in a green velvet jacket this morning. He also, Curtis could not help observing, wore trousers far too close-cut for what most people would call decency, the cloth tight on what was admittedly, but all too obviously, a well-shaped form. Good God, could the fellow be any more blatant about his tastes?

"Poetical art?" he repeated, and saw Holt's mock-despairing shake of the head.

"I have the honour to edit Edward Levy's latest volume." Da Silva paused invitingly. Curtis gave him a blank look. Da Silva raised his dark eyes heavenwards. "The Fragmentalist. The *poet*. You're not familiar—? Of course not. Ah, well, genius is not often recognised. And you may prefer to draw your intellectual sustenance from Mr. Kipling's barrack-room ballads, which are perhaps more to a man of action's taste. They *rhyme properly*, I'm so very often informed."

He waved a graceful hand at Lady Armstrong and drifted out, leaving Curtis staring open-mouthed.

"Of all the—" He stopped himself.

"Rotten dago queers," James Armstrong finished for him, with more accuracy than good manners. "I bar that man. Honestly, Sophie, why you have to invite him—"

"He's a poet himself, you know," said Lady Armstrong. "Terribly clever. So modern."

"He's terribly good looking too," Fenella Carruth offered, with a demure look at her companion. "Don't you think, Pat?"

"Handsome is as handsome does," said Miss Merton with severity. "Too flashy by half, if you ask me."

The walking party set off fortified by a huge breakfast, leaving Curtis and da Silva in possession of the house. Da Silva announced his intention of settling in the library to commune with his muse. Curtis, feeling sorry for the muse, said that he preferred to explore the house and acquaint himself with its features.

He did plan to explore, but it was not modern amenities that he was looking for.

Sir Hubert's study door was open. Curtis slipped in and turned the key in the door to lock himself inside. His heart was pounding and his mouth dry.

This wasn't his style of thing. He wasn't a spy, for God's sake, he was a soldier.

Or rather, he had been a soldier, till the guns blew up at Jacobsdal.

He walked to the desk, and almost gave up there and then as he saw what was on it: a silver-framed photograph of a smiling young man in the uniform of a British lieutenant. He recognised the features from the full-length oil that hung in the drawing room, next to a stunning John Singer Sargent portrait of the current Lady Armstrong. Sir Hubert's elder son, Martin, dead on the dry earth of the Sudan.

Surely a man who had lost his son to war could not have betrayed British soldiers. Surely.

Another painting of the dead man hung opposite Sir Hubert's desk, staring down on Curtis with a thoughtful smile. It was displayed between a simple watercolour of a woman that Curtis guessed to be Armstrong's first wife, and a pastel sketch of Sophie, Lady Armstrong. There didn't seem to be a picture of James.

He made himself move on. The desk drawers were all locked but the filing cabinet was not, so he flicked through files and folders with the fingers of his left hand, wondering what he was playing at as he did so.

Sir Hubert had been vastly enriched by the collapse of Lafayette's armament business after Jacobsdal, but that meant nothing. He was an arms manufacturer, after all, and there had been a war on; the business had to go somewhere. And of course Mr. Lafayette had wanted to shift the blame from his own factory, and the weight of the Jacobsdal deaths from his own shoulders. He had stood in Sir Henry Curtis's drawing room, unshaven, thin and desperate, and he had raved about sabotage and plots, betrayal and murder, and his body had been dredged from the Thames not two weeks afterwards. He had said nothing that could not have sprung from guilt and madness.

But if there was the slightest chance that Lafayette had told the truth, Curtis could not ignore it. He had to do this, even if he had no real idea what he was doing or what he was looking for, so he flicked through his host's private papers, his face hot with shame.

He spent as long as he dared in there, listening out for noises in the hallway or approaching servants, and it was with immense relief that he reached the bottom of the cabinet. There had been no evidence of anything untoward, simply bills and letters, the routine business of a wealthy man.

He searched around the office for keys to the desk, but came up blank. Sir Hubert doubtless kept them on his keychain. He wondered how he could get at them.

Well, there was nothing more doing here, unless he proposed to force the drawers like a common thief. He checked as best he could that he had left no trace of his interference, and went to the door, where he listened for footfalls outside. There was only silence. He unlocked the study door, slipped out, peering over his shoulder as he did it, and walked straight into somebody.

"Jesus!" he yelped.

"I fear not," said a silky voice, and Curtis realised that he had collided with da Silva. "Both Jewish, of course, but the resemblance ends there."

Curtis stepped back, away from him, and bumped into the doorframe. Da Silva, making very little effort to hide his amusement, moved out of his way with a show of elaborate courtesy. "Doing a spot of work, were you?" he enquired, glancing into their host's study.

"How's your muse?" Curtis retorted and stalked off, face flaming.

God, how embarrassing, and what miserable bloody luck. At least he'd only been spotted by that blasted Levantine. For all he knew, da Silva would see nothing unusual in exploring one's host's private rooms.

That was an appealing thought, but unlikely; even the most ill-bred commoner would wonder what he was playing at. The question was whether the fellow would mention it to anyone. Curtis would have to think up some explanation, in case.

He went up to his room, cursing da Silva, unsure what to do next. He supposed a real spy might pry into the Armstrongs' bedrooms, but the thought revolted him. He would have to look elsewhere.

After a few minutes to recover his composure, he went into the library, having first poked his head round the door to confirm it was empty. It was a spacious room, wood-panelled in the style of much older homes and rather dark. The upper bookshelves were lined with marshalled rows of leather-bound volumes with matching spines, the sets of reference works and unreadable academic studies that new money might buy to fill up the shelf space. The lower shelves, within reach, held complete sets of Dickens and Trollope, along with all the latest clever novels and a lot of sensational yellow-back fiction. There was only one painting here, a portrait of a boy aged about nine, holding a baby. Curtis supposed that would be Martin and James. If so, that was the first picture of James Curtis had seen; he wondered if the man hated sitting for portraits as much as he did himself.

As well as the bookshelves and some comfortable reading chairs, there were a couple of occasional tables topped with heavy-based electric lamps, and a desk. He checked its drawers and found nothing but blank stationery and writing materials.

He looked around, and noticed an unobtrusive door at the far end of the room, close-fitted into the panelling. It was in the middle of the wall, and a quick mental survey of the house's layout made him think it was likely to be an anteroom, rather than a passage leading anywhere. Might it be a private study? He tried the door handle. It was locked.

"My, you are curious," murmured a voice in his ear, and Curtis almost jumped out of his skin.

"Good God." He turned to face da Silva, who stood right behind him. The man must move like a cat. "Do you mind not sneaking up on a chap?"

"Oh, is it *me* who's sneaking? I had no idea."

That was a shrewd blow. Curtis set his jaw. "It's a fascinating house," he said, and watched the amused twitch of da Silva's mouth with impotent fury.

"That's document storage." Da Silva nodded helpfully at the door. "Sir Hubert keeps most of his private papers there, under lock and key."

"Very sensible," muttered Curtis, and heard the luncheon gong with relief.

Relief turned to dismay when he realised that da Silva would be eating with him. It appeared the fellow would be crawling round him all day at this rate.

"I hope your work went well," he managed, attempting to maintain a veneer of civility as they sat opposite one another, across a lavish spread.

"Moderately successful, thank you." Da Silva buttered a roll with great care. "How about yours?"

Curtis's breath hitched at that little dig. "I've merely been wandering round. Having a look at the place. Remarkable house."

"Isn't it." Da Silva was watching him as he spoke, his face impossible to read, and Curtis had to stop himself from shifting under his gaze.

He grabbed for the nearest serving dish and proffered it, in the hope of changing the subject. "Ham?"

"No, thank you."

"It's a jolly good one."

Da Silva blinked, slowly, like a lizard. "I dare say, but I fear I haven't converted since we last spoke."

"Con— Oh. Oh, I beg your pardon. I quite forgot you were a Jew."

"How refreshing. So few people do."

Curtis wasn't quite sure how he was meant to take that remark, but it scarcely mattered. His uncle Sir Henry was a devout Christian but a well-travelled man, and one of the strictest tenets of Curtis's upbringing had been that one never expressed disrespect for another man's faith. It was not a view shared by many of his peers, and Curtis didn't feel inclined to be conciliatory to the bloody man, but a principle was a principle.

"I beg your pardon," he repeated. "I didn't mean to offend you. Er, how about beef?" He lifted the plate apologetically and saw what looked like a glimmer of laughter in the dark eyes.

"Beef is quite acceptable, thank you." Da Silva accepted the offering with great gravity. "I'm not offended by ham, you understand, I simply don't eat it. The only meat that *offends* me is kidney, and that's for aesthetic reasons."

That was exactly the sort of pansyish remark Curtis would have expected of him. Much more so than that intense scrutiny earlier, or the series of well-targeted jabs. He was damned if he knew quite what to make of this.

"So, er, are you a religious man?" he tried.

"No, I couldn't claim to be that. I'm not terribly observant." Da Silva gave a sudden, feline smile. "Of my faith, that is. I'm quite observant in general."

Curtis was sure that was another dig, but da Silva didn't follow it up, returning his attention to his plate. Curtis took the opportunity to look him over. He was a handsome enough fellow, he supposed, if you could tolerate the type, with those deep, dark eyes, a full, well-shaped mouth, high cheekbones, and black brows that were almost too elegantly curved. Curtis wondered if he did something to shape them and decided that he did. He had seen that sort in London, passing certain clubs: plucked eyebrows, powdered faces, rouged cheeks, chattering to one another in that affected way. Was that what da Silva did in his private hours, with other men?

Da Silva gave a slight cough and Curtis realised he had said something. "I beg your pardon, what was that?"

"I enquired as to your plans for the afternoon. Or shall we simply keep, ah, bumping into one another?"

"I shall go for a short walk in the grounds, I expect," Curtis snapped.

Da Silva's lips curved in a secret smile, as if relishing a joke that Curtis did not share. "I'll be in the library. Don't let me stand in your way."

That night, Curtis waited for the clock to strike one before he slipped out of his bedroom. The corridors were very dark, but he had checked his way and felt sure he could avoid knocking over any stuffed birds, occasional tables or other clutter.

He felt very heavy on his feet as he went down the stairs. There was no sign of life in the house. The servants would all be asleep, the guests who weren't asleep would be otherwise occupied.

He made it to the library without incident, though his blood was pounding in his ears, and shut the door with great care behind him. The room was shuttered for the night and it was pitch dark. He opened the slide of his dark lantern, letting out a beam of yellow light that made the silence and the dark close even more heavily around him.

He tried the door of the storage room to be sure it was still locked, and began to work through the ring of skeleton keys that he had bought, with appalling self-consciousness, in the East End.

One after another failed to fit, until he had tried them all. He cursed under his breath, then stiffened as he heard a sound. Very slight but—

It was a creak. Someone was opening the door.

Curtis moved without having to think, shutting the lantern slide to cut off the light and stepping as silently as he could to one side of the storage room door. He closed his fingers round the skeleton keys, knowing he had to get them into his pockets before they were seen, and without the slightest clink—

Whoever had opened the door had not switched on the light.

He could see the faintest glimmer of less than absolute dark from the hall around the doorframe. It was cut off as the door was closed without sound, and then a narrow beam of faint, whitish light cut through the middle of the room as the intruder, the *other* intruder, lit some device.

Someone was sneaking around with a torch.

It had to be a burglar. Of all the rotten luck. He would have to confront the fellow; he could hardly stand by and see his host robbed. There would be noise, it would raise the house, and he had skeleton keys in his pocket and a dark lantern by his side. Could he blame the burglar for those when help came?

The burglar moved forward in total silence, progress only indicated by the movement of the light. He was coming towards the storage-room door at the back of the library, where Curtis stood. A little closer, and he could spring on the fellow. He readied himself for action.

The light travelled up, over the desk, and stopped with a jerk on the dark lantern that Curtis had left there. He tensed, and the light swung round and beamed directly into his face.

Shocked, blinded but unhesitating, Curtis launched himself forward, left fist leading into—nothing, because the intruder wasn't there. He heard the faintest whisper of movement, and a hand was clapped over his mouth, warm fingers pressing against his lips.

"Dear me, Mr. Curtis," murmured a voice in his ear. "We really must stop meeting like this."

Curtis froze, then as the smooth hand moved from his mouth, he hissed, "What the devil are you playing at?"

"I might ask you the same." Da Silva was right behind him, body pressed close, and his free hand slid, shockingly intimate, over Curtis's hip.

He shoved a vicious elbow back, getting a satisfying grunt from da Silva as he made contact, although not as hard as he'd have liked, but when he turned and grabbed where his opponent should have been, he found only empty space. He glared into the dark, frustrated.

"Well, well." Da Silva's low voice came from a few steps away. The little light flicked on again. Curtis moved towards it, intending violent retribution, and stopped short as he saw what it was illuminating. His skeleton keys, in da Silva's hand.

"You picked my bloody pocket!"

"*Quiet.*" The beam of light flickered off the keys, around the room and over the desk. "Don't shout, and please don't start a fight. Neither of us wants to be caught."

Enragingly, that was true. "What are you doing in here?" demanded Curtis, trying to keep his voice as low as da Silva's murmur.

"I was going to break into Sir Hubert's storage room. And, given the skeleton keys and dark lantern, I think you had the same idea."

Curtis opened and shut his mouth in the darkness. He managed, "Are you a thief?"

"No more than you. I suspect we may have shared interests, unlikely as that may seem."

"It seems damned unlikely to me!"

"And this *is* likely?" Da Silva beamed his light at the dark lantern. "Archibald Curtis, late of His Majesty's service, a *Boy's Own Paper* reader if ever I saw one—a burglar? I don't think so. I certainly hope not. You're dreadful at it."

Curtis seethed. "Whereas you're a natural, I suppose."

"Keep your voice down." Da Silva's voice was only just audible, entirely controlled.

"Give me one reason I shouldn't raise the house," Curtis said through his teeth.

"If you were going to, you'd have done it already. Two choices, Mr. Curtis. Do the decent thing, shout for help, and watch me spoil your plans while you spoil mine. Or..."

"Or what?"

He could hear the purr in da Silva's voice. "Or I could open that door."

Curtis didn't reply, because he could think of nothing to say. Da Silva went on. "If we have common interests, we'll find out when we're in there. If we don't, well, I shan't stand in your way and I trust you won't stand in mine. If neither of us finds what we seek, we'll apologise to our host in thought, and pretend this never happened. But all of that depends on getting through that door. What do you say?"

It was outrageous. He ought to tell him to go to the devil. It was unthinkable that he should ally himself to this bounder.

What he said was, "Can you open it?"

"Probably. May I?" Da Silva moved to the dark lantern and flicked the slide to shed light on the door lock. He handed the flashlight to Curtis as though they were regular partners. "Take this and listen out."

Da Silva dropped to his knees by the door, silhouetted in the light from the dark lantern. Curtis bent closer and saw he was manipulating long, slender pieces of metal.

"Are you picking that lock?" he demanded.

"Is that worse than using skeleton keys?"

"You *are* a thief!"

"On the contrary." Da Silva sounded unruffled. "My father's a locksmith. I learned his trade in my cradle. Some day I shall give you his views on the uselessness of skeleton keys. I trust you didn't pay too much for them."

Curtis bit back an angry response, knowing it would be bluster. Da Silva's slim fingers moved, steady, skilful and unhurried.

The house was silent, only his own breathing audible. Feeling useless, Curtis flicked on the flashlight, admiring the strength of its beam. The newfangled things tended to be weak and unreliable, but this was an impressive piece of kit; he should like to examine it when he had a chance. He played the light over the door, checking for other locks or bolts in lieu of anything better to do, and his eyes widened as the light caught something that he hadn't noticed before.

"Da Silva," he hissed.

"Busy."

"*Da Silva.*" Curtis grabbed his shoulder, digging his fingers in. The dark head swung round, black eyes unfriendly.

"What?"

"That." Curtis circled the light on his discovery.

"*What?*"

Da Silva was still on the floor, holding his picks in the lock, looking up at the unobtrusive metal plate on the door with no sign of understanding. Curtis knelt to bring their heads level, and felt a stab of pain and weakness in his kneecap as his leg bent. He grabbed for da Silva's shoulder to steady himself, leaning on the kneeling man, and heard him give a very slight grunt of effort as he took Curtis's weight.

Curtis lowered himself to the floor, hand still gripping the slender shoulder that seemed stiff with effort or tension, and whispered into da Silva's ear, feeling the warmth of his own breath bounce off the skin so close to his mouth. "Wire running to the door. Metal plate on the frame and the door. It's an electrical contact. If you open the door, you'll break the circuit."

"Meaning?"

"I think it might be an alarm."

Da Silva's body went rigid under Curtis's hand. "Well," he breathed. "How thrillingly modern. Doesn't want us to get in there, does he?"

Curtis would have voiced a strong objection to "us", but that was drowned in the rush of sensation along his nerves. If Sir Hubert was really hiding something... If Lafayette had been right...

If that was the case, no matter that the man was his host, and elderly. He would break his damned neck.

"Electricity is beyond my ken," da Silva murmured. "Do you know how to deal with that?"

Curtis inspected the metal plates. He would need to ensure the circuit didn't break when the door was opened, so...

"Yes. I'll need some kit."

"Can you get it?"

"Not now."

Da Silva let out an audible exhalation. "When?"

"Tomorrow night. But we talk first. I want to know what you're up to."

"We established that. The same as you."

"We talk first," Curtis repeated, pressing his advantage. "Or I'll go to Sir Hubert, and the devil with the consequences."

Da Silva opened his mouth, clearly decided not to argue, and gave him a malevolent look. "Fine. Tomorrow."

"Can you lock it again?"

Da Silva shot him an irritated glance in lieu of answer. He was busy for a few more seconds then withdrew the picks. "Very well, that was a waste of a night. Let's go. You first, and don't forget your things."

Curtis crept up the stairs, dark lantern in hand, keys in pocket. He was in his room, undressing as quietly as possible, when he heard the click of a door in the corridor. He felt a pulse of alarm and then realised that it must be da Silva going to his own room.

Of course the man would be his neighbour. Naturally. It would be nice, he thought with justified irritation, if Fate could stop throwing that limp-wristed thieving bloody dago in his way.

Chapter Three

The next morning, there was no sign of da Silva while Curtis breakfasted. Holt was there, full of morning exuberance. He gave Curtis a cheerful greeting that lifted his spirits somewhat; at least there was one person at Peakholme he could enjoy spending time with.

They chatted inconsequentially for a few moments, moving back to sporting talk. Holt enquired, "I say, can you spar any more? I wondered if you might like to go a few rounds."

It hurt to shake his head to that. "Not really. Maybe in a few years. I still have the knuckles, but it's a little painful. And the knee slows me down."

"That's a damned thing. You had a wonderful right."

Boxing was the smallest part of what Curtis had lost at Jacobsdal. "There's men worse off." He managed a smile. "Otherwise I should have given you a run for your money."

"I'm jolly sure of that. What do you say to a spot of billiards instead? If you can play, that is." Holt flushed. "I didn't think—I beg your pardon. Stupid of me."

"Not at all. I manage fairly well, actually, and I'll be pleased to prove it to you." Curtis was a natural left-hander. He'd had the tendency beaten out of him at school, of course, but it meant that Jacobsdal had not entirely deprived him of skill. "I might take a turn in the grounds first, though, I'd like some fresh air."

"I'll beg your escort then, Mr. Curtis," said Fenella Carruth from across the table. "I shan't hurry you, don't worry. Pat likes to march but I'd far rather stroll."

"I shall march ahead and meet you at the folly," Miss Merton told her.

Curtis gave a polite smile, trying not to show his tension. He needed to speak to da Silva, not to socialise, and apparently the fellow was recouping his energies from last night by lounging in bed. The unspeakable creature.

He strolled with Miss Carruth through the emergent woods and gardens round Peakholme. The planting had begun early in the project, so that the trees were well established, and the paths were laid out with care and thought.

"This is a wonderful place," said Miss Carruth. "So full of interest, and the grounds will be marvellous when everything's bedded in."

"In a hundred years' time?"

"Quite." She gave her gurgling laugh. "Have you been to the folly yet?"

Curtis felt as though everything to do with Peakholme was a folly, but he suffered Miss Carruth to lead him through the grounds, a good few minutes' walk into young woodland, crunching through autumn leaf fall until they came out into a clearing that sloped up to the top of a ridge. Looking up, Curtis saw a round grey stone tower at the crest of the slope, dominating the view. The style of building suggested it was about eight centuries older than Peakholme. It seemed to be a defensive outpost of some sort, but Curtis assessed the ground with a soldier's eye, and couldn't see anything worth defending in the rocky slopes around them.

As they approached the folly, he saw Miss Merton, standing with her shoulders set and arms folded. He thought for a second that the man with her, silhouetted against the bright grey sky, might be Holt, but the languid stance was nothing like Holt's solid, foursquare way of holding himself, and he realised it was da Silva, his slim form muffled under a bulky overcoat.

"Uh-oh, that looks like trouble brewing. Hello, Pat," Miss Carruth called, striding up the slope a little faster. "Am I late?"

"Miss Merton and I have been having the most delightful intimacy," purred da Silva. Curtis took one glance at Miss Merton's rigid expression, and turned swiftly to contemplate the view.

"Let's take a proper walk, Fen," Miss Merton said. "I need some fresh air."

Curtis seized his opportunity. "Then I'll leave you ladies to it. I'm afraid my knee won't bear much more, and I'd like a look at the folly."

"Alas, I had hoped to commune in solitude with my muse," da Silva murmured mournfully. "I might as well have gone to Piccadilly Circus."

Curtis caught Miss Merton's eye in brief, heartfelt agreement on Mr. da Silva and his muse. "Well, I dare say I won't bother you long. See you later, Miss Merton, Miss Carruth."

As the two women departed, da Silva went to open the oak door of the folly. He made an inviting gesture. Curtis, already stepping forward, was struck with a sudden hesitation, glancing round.

The ladies wouldn't think this was some sort of...assignation, would they? Curtis slipping off to a remote place with a fellow like da Silva...

He shook himself at the absurdity. Nobody would think such a thing of him, even if it would be the obvious conclusion to reach about da Silva, and even if they did, *he* knew he was about no such business.

He strode through the doorway, glancing at the heavy door that da Silva held open. Its style suggested great age, but it showed no more sign of weathering or dilapidation than the stone blocks around it.

"Did Sir Hubert put this thing in?" Curtis wondered aloud as da Silva shut the door, enclosing them in the stone space. It was bare but for a couple of heavy wooden chests against the walls. The mullioned glass of the windows was secure and, he was sure, wrong for the building's appearance. There were some steps up the side of the wall to a mezzanine floor, laid in new oak.

"Of course he did." Da Silva led the way up the stairs. "He commissioned it as a brand new piece of antiquity. Shockingly vulgar."

That from a man wearing an absurdly foppish velvet jacket and those appallingly tight trousers. Curtis wondered why a fellow would want to draw attention to himself so. "Well, you should know," he retorted.

"Oooh. Harsh." Da Silva sounded unruffled. "Restore your offended sensibilities with the view." He indicated the astonishing vista over the Pennine slopes. "The single advantage of this ridiculous building. It helps that while one is *in* the folly, one can't actually *see* it."

That was quite enough of architecture, Curtis felt. "Let's get to brass tacks. I want to know what's going on."

"I'm not inclined to tell you that yet."

Curtis drew a breath. "Listen—"

Da Silva swung to face him, dark eyes intent. "Who are you working for?"

"What?"

"I said, who are you working for? It's not a difficult question."

"I'm not working for anyone."

Da Silva exhaled dramatically. "Let us not beat about the bush. You're a gentleman, not a player. You're not a habitual thief. And you are the nephew of Sir Maurice Vaizey, chief of the Foreign Office Private Bureau. Did he send you here?"

"What? No, he did not. How the devil do you know he's my uncle?"

Da Silva's perfect eyebrows contracted into a frown. "We've limited time, don't play the fool. Just tell me, are you here on Vaizey's behalf? About the blackmail, or anything else?"

"What blackmail?" Curtis was hopelessly confused now. "I don't know what you mean. I don't know anything about any blackmail and I don't suppose my uncle has any idea I'm here."

Da Silva's dark eyes were on his face, reading it. He said, slowly, "If you aren't here about that... You were wounded at Jacobsdal. Lafayette's business collapsed because of what happened there, and Armstrong made a fortune. Is that it? Something to do with Jacobsdal?"

Curtis took a stride forward, fist clenching. "If you know anything about that—"

"Nothing whatsoever. I'm here about something else."

"Then why did you say our interests might coincide?"

Da Silva shrugged with some irritation. "I was wrong. It was one o'clock in the morning. Forgive me for not divining your purpose on the spot."

Curtis glowered at him. "Well, what's *your* purpose? What's this about blackmail?"

Da Silva didn't answer that. He was watching Curtis, weighing something up. When he spoke, it was with care, but little trace of the mannered drawl. "Mr. Curtis, I need, probably more urgently than you, to get into the private rooms and papers here. It is of some importance that you do not get in my way or arouse suspicion. Two of us playing the same game will double the risks for us both. Could I persuade you to enlighten me on dealing with the alarm, and then leave this business to me?"

"No."

"I can look for information as well as you can, and probably with rather more subtlety. Suppose you tell me what you're after, and I pass you whatever I find—"

"What do you know about armaments, or sabotage?" The banked rage that never stopped smouldering leapt into life. "What do you know about war?"

Da Silva pressed his lips tight. "Granted, I'm not a military man—"

"I lost friends at Jacobsdal. Good men. If Armstrong was responsible for sabotaging British guns for British troops—"

"Then he committed murder and treason," da Silva interrupted. "For which the penalty is a short drop and a lengthened neck. This may be a matter of life and death, Mr. Curtis. You will need to proceed with great caution."

"The only thing I've to be cautious about is you. What do you know, and what the devil are you up to? And what's this about blackmail? Someone's blackmailing you?"

"Oddly enough, no." Da Silva paused, considering, then spoke with sardonic precision. "There was another victim. A man with, ah, unusual tastes. He was bled dry with the threat of arrest and exposure, and when he had nothing more to give, he took the only way out left to him." Da Silva's lip curled. "He was not the sort of man to say publish and be damned, but nor was he altogether weak. He told me about the blackmail before he jumped from Beachy Head."

Curtis blinked. "Why you?"

"He was a...friend." Curtis thought he could guess what that meant. "And he told me that the compromising situation that ruined him occurred at Peakholme. What he did in this house was used to destroy him. He mentioned other names too, other guests, amongst whom there has been at least one other suicide. Two dead men, and they may only be the tip of a very sordid iceberg."

"But how would that happen? People are indiscreet at country houses all the time." He knew of houses where a bell was rung to give guests ten minutes to return to their own marital beds before morning tea was brought in. That wasn't his idea of entertainment, but it suited a great many people, and it was generally accepted, but never mentioned.

"There are different levels of indiscretion, of course."

"I suppose you mean queers." Curtis didn't like this sly, allusive way of speaking, mostly because he wasn't sure he could follow it. "You still can't blackmail a man to his death with gossip."

Da Silva gave him a curling smile. "Did you inspect your room closely?"

"How do you mean?"

"Anything strike you as odd about it, at all?"

"No. Why should it?" Curtis found Da Silva's tilted eyebrow an irritant.

"Not the layout?"

Curtis opened his mouth to respond, and stopped. It seemed absurd to complain about the rather awkward arrangement of the rooms, set in pairs and widely spaced along a long corridor. It was a modern house; they did things in modern ways. He was not going to argue about any such trivialities, anyway. "What are you getting at?"

"In your bedroom, there's a large mirror, hanging on the wall opposite the bed. The wall which backs onto a service area."

"And? Just a moment. Have you been in my bedroom?"

"My room is on the other side of the corridor from you. A mirror image of yours. Should you care to visit me, you'll observe that the large mirror in my room is also opposite the bed, also backing onto a service area." He gave Curtis a meaningful look.

Curtis said, with dawning incredulity, "Are you suggesting that's a two-way mirror?"

"There's one in every guest room, I suspect. If you lift the mirror in my room off the wall, first removing the screws that keep it in place, you can see a good-sized aperture through to a narrow dead-end passage that connects to the service corridor at the far end."

"You are bloody joking."

"No. If you can think of a reason to knock a hole in the wall and then put a mirror over it, except to put a camera behind the mirror, I'll be fascinated. Come to that, I can't imagine what else those hidden corridors were built for in the first place."

"Well...electricity—something to do with the heating..."

"It's possible. The most charitable interpretation is that they were adapted once our host realised the potential for blackmail, rather than built with it in mind. Either way, Armstrong is in this to the neck. Armstrong and his delightful house, so far from London, with such well-chosen guests and, I don't know if you've noticed, some very attractive and attentive servants. The young blond who showed me to my room was particularly charming."

Curtis struggled for words. "Orchestrated, planned extortion?"

"Quite."

"Why?"

"Money." Da Silva spoke as though it were obvious.

"But Armstrong's rich!"

"Have you any idea how much this place cost to build? The folly, the redwood trees imported from Canada, the electrical wiring, the heating devices? The glass bulbs in the light fittings are especially manufactured for this house, in vast quantity. They have their own custom telephone exchange, and an electrical generator that runs off water, all built for Peakholme.

It takes a king's ransom to keep it running, and talking of costing a fortune, Lady Armstrong and the egregious James are extravagant to a fault. Her patronage of the arts—she's delightfully kind to struggling poets—and her dresses. His horses and gambling, and he's bone idle, lives off his father and doesn't lift a finger. Armstrong's business is sound enough, but he's spending to the top of his bent. He needs another war; short of that, he needs money."

Curtis frowned. "How do you know all this? How sure are you?"

"About his financial worries? I've heard plenty of whispers. About the blackmail—well, I'll be certain when I find where he keeps the photographic evidence. Until then it's hearsay, guesswork and deduction. But I should scarcely have come to the countryside, in October of all times, for anything less than profound concern. Those are my cards on the table, Mr. Curtis. I believe that Armstrong is engaged in a cruel and deliberate scheme of entrapment and blackmail that has driven men to their deaths. What do you believe?"

It was Curtis's turn to examine the other man's face now. Could he trust da Silva? He seemed sincere, as far as Curtis could tell. And God knew, he needed help.

He took a deep breath. "Lafayette came to my uncle's house about a month ago."

"Which uncle?"

"Sir Henry. He'd been to see Sir Maurice already, at his office. Sir Maurice sent him packing, so he came to appeal to Sir Henry. Because of this, I suppose." He lifted his damaged hand. "He hoped Sir Henry might speak to Sir Maurice."

"Do you always address your uncles as Sir What-have-you?" da Silva put in curiously.

"Yes, why not?" Sir Henry Curtis and Sir Maurice Vaizey, his father's and mother's brothers, had been responsible for Curtis's rearing. Sir Henry had remained unmarried through

Curtis's childhood; Sir Maurice had been a widower for decades. Curtis had never doubted their affection, but his upbringing hadn't been sentimental.

Da Silva shrugged. "Why not indeed. Of course. Carry on."

Curtis bristled, sensing an implied criticism without quite knowing what it was. But da Silva was twitching a finger as if to hurry him on. He got back to the point. "Sir Henry's in Africa, though, and I was there, so Lafayette talked to me instead. He'd broken down, he was half-starved and raving, for all I know it was pure madness. Sir Maurice certainly thought so. But he, Lafayette, said that Armstrong had sabotaged his factory. That Armstrong had engineered the flaws in the new guns to destroy Lafayette's business and take his share."

"What made his claim credible?"

"I don't know if it is. He believed that two of his most trusted men, a foreman and a clerk, had been suborned by Armstrong to sabotage him. He said they'd both vanished. I checked that, they've both been reported missing by their families."

"What do you think happened to them?"

"I've no idea. Lafayette suspected foul play, but he didn't know for sure. They might just as well have taken a bribe and left the country. If any of this happened at all."

"If I suborned men to commit an act of high treason, I should probably silence them afterwards," said da Silva thoughtfully. "But then, if I committed high treason, I should leave the country sharpish, so who can say. What happened to Lafayette? Did someone say he died?"

"About a fortnight after I spoke to him. A couple of weeks ago now. He was found in the Thames. It seems he hit his head and fell into the river."

"Hit his head," da Silva repeated.

"Yes."

"Did anyone wonder if someone hit his head for him?"

Curtis had wondered that since reading the inquest report. He felt a rush of warmth for da Silva, sheer relief at sharing his thoughts. "Impossible to tell. The body was in the river for a couple of days before it was found. The coroner called it an accident."

"He'd started to talk and then he was found in the river with a smashed head." Da Silva made a face. "So you are here to establish if there's any truth in what may have been the ranting of a disturbed man, or the discoveries of a wronged and perhaps murdered one. Well, now we know where we stand. Do we make common cause?"

That wasn't, on the face of it, an attractive prospect. But Curtis stood no chance at all of finding anything out alone, whereas da Silva seemed to have a fair idea what he was about, and could at least pick locks. And Curtis needed those doors opened, needed to know if he had lost his friends, his career, his purpose in life to treason rather than malignant fate. Come to that, he needed to know if da Silva was right about mirrors in the rooms and men driven to their deaths, because if that was the case, whatever else he was or was not guilty of, Armstrong deserved horsewhipping and Curtis would damned well make sure he got it.

Subterfuge did not come easily to Curtis. Just now, he could use a man like da Silva. And, while he'd already realised that da Silva's effeminate mannerisms concealed sharp eyes and a sharper mind, it seemed that he had courage, too, and even a sense of decency. Curtis had an uncomfortable feeling that he might have judged him rather ungenerously.

"Very well. Common cause."

He held out his right hand without thinking. Da Silva took it, with no obvious repugnance at the mutilation. His grip was light on Curtis's scars, but decidedly less flaccid than when they'd first shaken.

"Well, then, let us move on," da Silva said. "What do you need to deal with that alarm in the library?"

"Clips and wires. There are supplies in the house, Armstrong showed me the workroom yesterday. I'll see to it."

"Then I shall meet you at, shall we say, one a.m. in the library? I look forward to our assignation."

Chapter Four

It felt bizarre to return to the party after that. At luncheon, Mrs. Lambdon and Mrs. Grayling wanted to know all about his uncle; as ever, the legend of the tall, handsome explorer cast a glamour over his family. Curtis fielded the familiar questions, mind elsewhere.

The conversation in the folly seemed unreal now, especially with da Silva every sinuous inch the effete aesthete once more, making dramatic, fluttery remarks that set the women giggling and the men rolling their eyes in disdain. Had he really shaken hands with him on a deal to burgle their host?

And could da Silva be right? Who the devil was being blackmailed here? Surely not the Lambdons, they were Lady Armstrong's family. The Graylings? They were wealthy, and he had thought Mrs. Grayling had a wandering eye. Miss Carruth? It couldn't be. Had Armstrong hoped to blackmail *him*? With what?

After luncheon, he took refuge in the unoccupied library to avoid James Armstrong's offers of sporting activity and Mrs. Grayling's sly over-friendliness. The selection of yellow-back novels included a wide range of mysteries and romps by Edgar Wallace and E. Phillips Oppenheim, all packed with gentleman spies, mysterious foreigners and sultry seductresses. Curtis enjoyed that sort of thing, but he couldn't make himself fancy the idea today. The actual life of a gentleman spy, it seemed to him, consisted of sneaking about, breaking the rules of hospitality and generally being anything but a gentleman, and the only mysterious foreigner around was da Silva. He was probably the closest thing Peakholme had to offer to a sultry seductress, come to that.

Da Silva would be the villain if this were an Oppenheim story. Curtis wished he was the villain now. He did not want to find out that Sir Hubert was a blackmailer, still less a traitor, that his host had cost Curtis his hand and George Fisher his life...

He stopped that thought in its tracks before the anger came back, and made himself look at the library shelf. As he examined the books, a name on a narrow spine snagged his attention.

He pulled out a slim volume, plainly bound in grey, and there it was. *The Fish-pond. Poems by Daniel da Silva.*

This, he had to see.

Curtis took a comfortable leather chair and opened the book at random. After a few minutes, bewildered, he went back to the beginning and started there.

He was not a man for poetry. He could tolerate Tennyson, the shorter pieces, and he liked some of the stirring stuff that everyone knew, like "Invictus", or the one that went "Play up! Play up! and play the game", even if talk of sands sodden red with blood seemed rather less poetic once one had seen the reality of it. A few of the men in South Africa had recited some of Mr. Kipling's things in camp during the long evenings, and they were jolly entertaining, with proper rhymes, as if there was anything wrong with that, and a good beat, and a story that a chap could follow.

Da Silva's poems were not like that.

They were broken fragments, not even sentences. They went...somewhere, that was clear, but the words twined round each other and broke off and led to conclusions Curtis didn't reach but which he could feel pressing down on him, unwholesome and disturbing. There were vivid images, but they were extraordinary ones, not poetic at all in the way Curtis vaguely felt poetry should be, with trumpets or mountains or daffodils. These poems were full of broken glass and water—which was not clean water—and scaly things that moved in the dark. There was a recurring image that seemed to sum it all up somehow, of a thing in the depths. Curtis couldn't quite tell what it was. It came in a bright flash of scales, a dark gleam, or a slither against an unwary hand, and vanished again, but it was always lurking, just out of reach, waiting.

He turned back to the opening pages and read the epigraph, a quote attributed to "Webster".

When I look into the fish-ponds in my garden
Methinks I see a thing armed with a rake
That seems to strike at me.

When he looked up from the book again, da Silva was leaning against the bookshelves, watching him.

"I, er," said Curtis, with the natural awkwardness of an Englishman caught reading poetry. "I just, er, picked this up." He wondered how long the other man had been there, and how he moved so silently.

"That's what it's for," da Silva agreed. "I shan't embarrass you by asking for an opinion."

Under normal circumstances Curtis would have liked nothing less than to be solicited for his opinion on poetry, but that stung. He might not be a literary type but he wasn't a bloody fool, and his mind was full of unsettling things that swam in dark water.

"I didn't understand it. I dare say I'm not meant to." He saw the droop of da Silva's eyelids and added, before the man could get in another dig at his philistinism, "Reminded me of Seurat, actually."

Da Silva's face went blank. "Of—?"

He'd wrong-footed the blighter, Curtis realised with immense satisfaction. "Seurat. The Impressionist," he explained. "Chap who paints pictures with dots."

Da Silva's eyes narrowed to black slits. "I know who Seurat is. Why should my poetry remind you of him?"

He looked, for a second, just a touch defensive, not quite as self-possessed as usual, and on the instant Curtis thought that if he wrote poetry he wouldn't much want people making cutting remarks about it. Especially not stuff like this, which seemed to be dredged up in pieces from the bottom of the writer's mind. He had no idea what *The Fish-pond* told him about Daniel da Silva but he felt, instinctively, that it contained something from under the hard exterior shell, something raw, that flinched when touched.

"Seurat's paintings," he said, feeling his way to his own meaning. "If you look at them they're just dots of colour, a lot of jumbled bits that don't make any sense. If you stand back far enough, it comes together and becomes a whole picture. That's what I thought about this." He glanced at the book in his hand and added, "I think I'd need to be a bit further away to grasp it, mind you. Manchester, perhaps."

Da Silva looked startled for a second, then his face lit with a smile. It was perhaps the first genuine, unstudied expression Curtis had seen from him, a combination of surprise, amusement and pleasure that made him look suddenly alive, and younger, too, without the world-weary pose. The thought came to Curtis, unbidden, that Miss Carruth had been right. Daniel da Silva was rather handsome.

"That's the most cogent analysis I've heard in a while," da Silva said. "You should review for *The New Age*."

That was one of those modern, socialist, intellectual periodicals. Curtis had never picked it up in his life, as da Silva would doubtless have guessed. "Oh, above my touch," he retorted. "Perhaps the *Boy's Own Paper* needs a poetry critic."

Da Silva laughed out loud. "An excellent idea. 'In this issue: How to tie reef knots; thrilling tales of war; and Writing the Sonnet with General Gordon.'"

Curtis was laughing too. "'Broken Down: A boy's adventure among the Fragmentalists.'"

Da Silva snorted inelegantly, shoulders shaking. Curtis felt rather pleased to be holding his own against the other man's quicksilver wit. He hadn't noticed anyone else at this party making da Silva laugh.

He grinned, and da Silva smiled back, and then the smile faded, and tilted, and now it wasn't boyish any more. It was...intimate. Inviting. And this was not Curtis's line at all, but even he could see that the dark eyes on his were taking him in, the gaze sliding over him with clear appreciation.

He was alone in a room with a chap who preferred men, and the fellow was *looking* at him.

Curtis couldn't think of a damned thing to say.

Da Silva's mouth curled in that secret smile of his, enjoying a joke that nobody else could hear. He began, "You know," pushing himself forward from his lounging stance, then looked round quickly as the door opened.

"There you are, Curtis." Holt and Armstrong clattered in. "What say that game of billiards?"

Neither man included da Silva in the invitation, but he was already drifting over to another set of bookshelves, light on his feet as ever, features blank, oblivious to everyone present.

"What the devil's that?" demanded Armstrong, prodding at the book on the arm of Curtis's chair. "Poetry? Good God, you aren't reading that tripe, are you? *The Fish-pond?*" he read out with heavy contempt. "What rubbish. Oh, I say." He'd clearly registered the author's name. "Let's have a look."

If Curtis wanted to see bullying, he'd go back to school. He pushed himself upright, swiped the book from Armstrong's fingers before he could open it, and limped over to return it to the shelf, feeling the stiffness in his knee that came after sitting for too long. He flexed his leg with annoyance. "If you're after a game, let's play."

He didn't know if he was anticipating one o'clock or dreading it. Both, perhaps. He went up to his room early with a plea of tiredness, needing to get away from the boisterous young men who proposed game after game of billiards, bridge or whist, and lay on his bed fully clothed. He was uncomfortably aware of the mirror that occupied so much of the wall opposite, its blankness gazing down on him.

Was there someone watching him now? No, that would be absurd. But he couldn't help thinking of the pretty maid who he had surprised in his room earlier that evening. Was that chance, or had she been waiting for him? Or if Mrs. Grayling's smiling flirtatiousness had caught his interest? Would someone be watching then?

The party broke up downstairs around half past eleven. By a quarter to one, the house was silent. Curtis waited a few minutes more, then had to go before his nerves got the better of him. Clad in black trousers and a dark pullover under his navy dressing gown, dark lantern in hand and wires in his pocket, he slipped down the stairs as silently as he could.

He examined the storeroom door to satisfy himself his planned rig-up would work, then waited in the library for a couple of minutes, tense and impatient, not sure if he should start without da Silva, or if he should be here at all. What if this was some sort of scheme? What if da Silva couldn't be trusted? What if his host came down and saw him, here— He shuddered at the thought.

In the hall and over the house, clocks let out a single chime, and the door slid open with a whisper of air. Try as he might, Curtis could barely hear da Silva's footfall as he slipped in.

Da Silva shut the library door before switching on the flashlight. "Hello," he murmured. "Ready? Very well. Shall I pick the lock first or will you need to do your electrical wizardry?"

"Can you pick the lock without opening the door? Good, then do that. Don't open it, even a little."

"Understood. You watch for the hall. Listen out."

Curtis nodded, and held out the dark lantern to his partner in crime. He stood sentry, in the dark, listening for noise in the hall, watching the deft, precise movements of da Silva's hands in the pool of light surrounding the lock, since he could see nothing else. In just a couple of moments, he heard a quiet click.

"All yours," da Silva said softly. "I'll watch out."

Curtis made his way over, feeling like some great galumphing beast next to his light-footed companion. It was the work of moments to attach the wire he'd taken from a workroom to the contacts with the putty he had also picked up, ensuring that the circuit would remain connected.

"What's that?" Da Silva spoke close to Curtis's ear, breath tickling his cheek, making him jump.

"God's sake," he hissed. "Make some damned noise, can't you?"

"Certainly not. What is it?"

"I've rigged a wire. It'll keep the circuit complete, I hope. It's long enough to maintain the connection as we open the door. Just don't dislodge it."

"I see. You, ah, 'hope'?"

"I can't guarantee there's nothing on the other side."

"Ah. Oh well, nothing ventured. May I?"

"Carefully."

Curtis took the flashlight and kept its beam on the putty and wire jury-rig as da Silva pulled the storeroom door open, as far as the wire would allow. No alarms sounded that he could hear. He let out a breath.

"Good work," murmured da Silva. "Right. Coming in?"

He slipped through the gap. Curtis, much bulkier, edged through, shut the door behind him, and opened the dark lantern slide as far as it would go to illuminate the scene. It was a small room with no windows and no exits. There were a few stacked chairs, a table, and a large wooden cabinet. He pulled at the top drawer, which was locked.

"Excuse me." Da Silva pierced the lock with a slender piece of metal, and wiggled it. There was, almost at once, a click. He pulled open the top drawer. "You take this, I'll do the bottom one, and we'll meet in the middle?"

Curtis nodded. Da Silva produced a second flashlight and closed the lantern slide again, so that the only illumination came from each man's torch. He dropped casually to a crouch and pulled open the lowest drawer.

Uncomfortably aware of da Silva at his feet, Curtis began to flick through the hanging files. Within a few seconds, he came across photographic prints. He pulled one out, and his mouth went dry.

"Look."

Da Silva straightened up so he stood next to Curtis and looked at the image in the torchlight.

"Well. If one wanted to blackmail the lady, that would suffice. Put it back where you got it."

Curtis slid the picture back into place. Da Silva was already flicking through the next folder, and Curtis realised that he hadn't been first-time lucky. Every folder held something. He winced at the procession of images, some a little blurry, black, grey and white snapshots of pleasure or depravity.

"Christ!" he hissed as da Silva took out a photograph that made his guts turn over. "Put it away."

Da Silva didn't. He was peering at the image, and Curtis glared at him. "For God's sake. I *know* him. He was at Oxford a couple of years after me. Put it away."

"Which one do you know?"

"The one—underneath." The one on all fours, face contorted with pain or pleasure, shoulders gripped by the powerful man who knelt behind him.

"Who is he?"

"None of your business."

"Don't be bloody stupid. Who is he, or more to the point, what does he do?" There was nothing louche in da Silva's tone, rather a sharp urgency.

"Foreign Office," said Curtis reluctantly. "He's an under-secretary."

"How ironic." Da Silva's words were clipped. "Because he's under a secretary right there, or at least an attaché. The blond's in the Prussian embassy."

Curtis stared at the fair-haired Prussian, captured in the act as he took the other man with obvious roughness. He felt peculiar, intrusive, quivering with illicit sensation. "I don't think a Foreign Office man should be doing that with a Prussian diplomat."

"Nor do I." Da Silva dropped the photo back into place and started going through more folders. "Here's another one."

Curtis grabbed the photo, incredulous. "For the love of God. I know him as well. He was in my college. Belongs to my club."

"He belongs to a couple of mine, come to that. Not very discreet. Isn't he an equerry of His Majesty?" Curtis nodded. "*Most* indiscreet. Notice we can't see the other chap's face." The equerry was obviously thrusting into a male body, but the recipient had his head buried in the sheets. Da Silva frowned. "Blond. I wonder if that's the obliging footman."

"That fellow Wesley?" Curtis tried to call him to mind. "It could be, I suppose."

"And— Oh. Look."

Curtis looked at the photograph da Silva held out, a woman being enjoyed by, and taking a good deal of enjoyment from, a man with a Y-shaped scar on his shoulder. He didn't recognise her, but as his gaze moved from the man's body to his face, his mouth dropped open. "Isn't that Lambdon?"

"It is. And..." Da Silva flicked back to the beginning of the drawer and pulled out the first picture again. This photograph was framed so that the man in it was cut off at the neck, but da Silva's finger tapped the distinctive scar on his shoulder. "It looks like this is too. Mr. Lambdon taking a leading role."

"Sir Hubert can't be blackmailing his own brother-in-law!"

"What makes you think it's Lambdon being blackmailed? Come to that, what makes you think it's just Sir Hubert blackmailing? Look at these, Curtis." Da Silva swept his hand over the drawer of files. "How many Oxford contemporaries of yours have you seen in this lot, your time or younger?"

"Three." Two had been with men. The third was enjoying a meteoric rise in the Catholic Church, which would not be helped by the photograph of his copulation with a busty young woman.

"Who in this house went to Oxford a couple of years after you? Who would know the gossip? Who's best placed to invite these fearfully nice chaps for a spot of shooting, meet the pater?" Da Silva's quiet tone was a vicious parody of an upper-class accent.

"You can't mean James Armstrong."

"Look at who they are. Think. James invites the young Turks, the ones with burgeoning careers and everything to lose.

Sophie selects the ladies. Women talk, she'll know who's frustrated, who's open to suggestions. They target them, they invite them, and then the footman, or her charming brother, or the bloody Prussian Ambassador beds them. It's a family business."

Curtis thought about that, holding the torch while da Silva went through the next drawer at speed. It held a few more photos, people he didn't recognise, one an older man with a girl who looked no more than twelve, and then sheaves of paper. Da Silva flicked, then stopped as Curtis grabbed his hand.

"What?"

Curtis scrabbled back through the folder and found what had caught his eye. He pulled it out. A page of diagrams, bitterly familiar. He stared at it, blood pounding in his temples.

"What *is* it?"

Curtis licked his lips. "It's the schema for a Lafayette rifle." He took a deep breath, then went through the papers around it, one by one. "Architectural plans of the Lafayette factory. More specifications for guns. For—" He stopped and swallowed hard, holding out the page. "This one is the revolver I used at Jacobsdal."

"Oh God," da Silva said softly. "Curtis..."

"Why would Armstrong have these, locked away here? Unless—"

Those papers, in this secret cabinet of vileness, could mean only one thing. Jacobsdal had been no accident. The guns had been sabotaged in the factory. Sir Hubert Armstrong had murdered the soldiers of Curtis's company, his men, his friends, as surely as if he had pulled the triggers himself.

The papers rattled in his hand. Da Silva took them from him, his touch gentle. "I'm sorry."

"Armstrong betrayed us. He sent us to hell, for profit."

"Keep your voice down." Da Silva's hand closed on Curtis's shaking wrist, and he tilted the torch so both their faces were partly lit. "It is unspeakable, and I can't imagine how angry you are, but *keep quiet.*"

"I'm going to kill him." Curtis's voice rasped in his throat.

"You'll have to fight the hangman for the privilege. Sabotage of the British Army in time of war? He'll swing for treason."

"Christ." Curtis clenched his useless, mutilated hand in its black leather sheath. "I'm in the bastard's house. Eating his food. His *guest.*" He wanted to vomit up every meal he'd had here. He wanted to drag Sir Hubert out of bed and beat him to a bloody pulp.

"We'll make him pay. I swear to you, Curtis, we'll see him dead. Don't lose your head now." Da Silva held his gaze till Curtis gave a stiff nod. He kept his grip on Curtis's wrist for a moment longer, the slim fingers a steadying contact, then let go and went back to the drawer.

Curtis stood still, trying to control the rage that surged through him. He had not truly believed Lafayette, had acted on his words only because inaction was impossible, but now there was no doubt. The full scale of Armstrong's treachery unspooled in his mind: the dead men and the mutilated. George Fisher's bewildered face. His own empty, futureless life, without the army, without the purpose and companionship that had been all he ever wanted. All of it to light Sir Hubert's house with electricity, to keep Lady Armstrong in dresses and James in horses.

"Shit and derision." Da Silva's voice was quiet but very clear.

That jolted Curtis out of his trance of fury. "What is it?"

Da Silva jerked a paper at him. Curtis registered the letterhead, and *For your eyes only.* "That's Foreign Office. What the devil is that doing here?"

"Ask your old college friend with the Prussian in his arse." Da Silva's hands were moving very fast now, flicking through typed and handwritten sheets. "Uh-oh. Tell me, as a military man, what does this look like to you?"

"Army supply-line plans." Curtis could barely bring himself to look; they were stamped Top Secret. "What the devil—? Why does Armstrong have these?"

"Why do you think?" snapped da Silva.

"Foreign Office men. Blackmail. Is Armstrong selling State secrets?" A thought struck him, and he felt the nape of his neck prickle. "You said this morning that he needs another war."

Da Silva took a deep breath. Then he patted the papers back into their folders, smoothing the edges down where they had been disarranged. "We get out of here now. We close up, leaving no trace. And you keep your mouth *shut*. Not one look, not one word to betray what you know till we're out of this house. I don't care how angry you are. This cabinet has enough in it to hang the Armstrongs five times over, and we're in their house, outnumbered, and thirty miles from anywhere."

"You can't be serious."

"Can't I?" hissed da Silva. "High treason? State secrets? Lafayette found in the river after he asked for help? Oh, *hell*. When did they invite you, Curtis? Before or after Lafayette came to you?"

"After." Curtis felt a sudden prickle of alarm. "But Sir Hubert was at school with Sir Henry, my uncle. It didn't seem odd..." Except that he'd thought at the time that the invitation was a damned fortunate coincidence. "Do you think they invited me to find out what I knew?"

"I don't know. There's something else. Lafayette isn't the only man who's been found in the Thames with a broken head."

"What?"

"There was another victim. He got angry. He was deliberating whether to speak out, bring evidence of the blackmail to the authorities. Then he vanished, and his body was found a few days later, in the river, with a smashed skull. A street robbery gone wrong, the coroner decided."

"Christ. You think—"

"I do." Da Silva looked sour. "Lafayette and a blackmail victim in the river? Two more men vanished? Does that all sound like chance?"

"No," Curtis said heavily. "It doesn't."

"I think the Armstrongs have killed to protect their secrets, and we must assume they'll kill again. If we take this information out of here, the Armstrongs will swing. If they discover what we know, what choice have they but to silence us? And they hold all the cards while we're in this house. If you don't keep this quiet, we're both as good as dead."

Curtis frowned. "How many do you think we'd be facing? Just the Armstrongs, or—"

"Some of the servants too. I don't see how the game could be worked without extra manpower. It would be risky to involve too many of them, but—"

"You know a lot of the groundsmen are ex-army," Curtis said.

"I did not know that." Da Silva didn't look pleased to hear it.

"Sir Hubert's older son Martin died in the first Boer war. Sir Hubert took on all the local men from his company that he could, in his memory. He was telling me about it just yesterday." He'd talked at length, longingly, to Curtis about beloved, clever, much-missed Martin, a hero in his father's memory. As though the men at Jacobsdal hadn't had fathers to mourn them. "The army pension's not much to live on, and this is a better post than a factory. They're trained men, and they'll likely be loyal to their master. Whether they'd kill for him..."

61

Da Silva winced. "I suggest we avoid finding out. Let's not get caught."

"I warn you, I'm a damned poor hand at dissembling."

"Improve. We *must* get these papers to the authorities, and we can't do that from a shallow grave under the redwoods. You have to appear your normal self until we can leave here. Play billiards with James Armstrong, talk soldiering with Sir Hubert."

"I was invited for a fortnight," Curtis said. "I can't spend two weeks in this nest of vipers. Not with—" Not eating and chatting and socializing with the man who had murdered his comrades. The thought was intolerable, indecent. He felt stained even considering it.

Da Silva's gaze was intent on him. "You won't have to. I'll get you out of here as quick as I can without rousing suspicion. Leave it to me, Curtis. I'll think of something."

Curtis nodded, absurdly grateful for the unexpressed understanding in those dark eyes. "I...that is, thank you."

"Thank me when I've thought of it. We'll discuss it tomorrow, we've been here too long." He shut the last drawer as he spoke, locking the cabinet with the picks, and pocketed his flashlight. "All right, let's go."

Curtis turned to the door and pushed it open. On the other side, the connecting wire broke free from the putty on the contact plate. A light instantly illuminated the library, glaringly bright for dark-adapted eyes. Faintly, somewhere in the house, a bell began to ring.

Chapter Five

"*Shit*," Curtis said, scarcely believing what he had just done.

Da Silva stood quite still for a second. Then he pushed Curtis into the library, following him, and shut the storeroom door behind them. "Hide the dark lantern, behind those books on the shelf. Quick, man."

"Shouldn't we run?"

"Don't argue." Da Silva grabbed the wire and putty off the doorframe and shoved them in his pocket, then dropped to the keyhole, working his picks with maddening deliberation. "And take off that pullover, just throw it over that chair. *Now.*"

Red with shame and anger at himself, Curtis did as he was told, pulling his dressing gown over his bare chest at da Silva's rapid, bewildering directions. There were running footsteps audible now. Several men, approaching fast.

"Over here, quick." Da Silva rose and turned his back to the storeroom door. Curtis stepped over, and da Silva said, urgently, "Don't hit me."

"Wh—"

Da Silva fisted his hands in Curtis's dressing gown, dragged him forward and kissed him on the mouth.

Curtis couldn't even react for a second. His mind was already fizzing with hurry, panic, anger at himself and rage at his traitorous host, the late hour and confusion, and now there was the sensation of hard lips battering his mouth, a hand behind his head, pulling at his hair and forcing his face forward, stubble that rasped across his skin. He stood, frozen stiff, and da Silva kicked his ankle viciously so that Curtis half-fell forward, leaning against him, and the main light clicked on, shocking him with its glare.

Da Silva pushed Curtis away so hard he stumbled a few paces back. He swung round to face three shotguns.

Fighting instinct surged, the appalling awareness of being unarmed and outnumbered overriding any other thoughts. He tensed, assessing the threat.

Three men in nightgowns. One was the handsome servant Wesley; the other two were both older, both with the unmistakable stamp of the soldier. All had their weapons—the latest model of heavy-duty Armstrong shotguns—at their shoulders, and all three had them aimed at Curtis. The older men were giving him their full attention, but Wesley was glancing over Curtis's shoulder, his eyes widening, biting back a smirk.

A few endless seconds ticked by as they stared at each other. They weren't about to shoot, Curtis registered.

"Put those guns down," he ordered. "Good work, but no need for it. Mr. da Silva and I were just—" He looked round as he spoke, indicating da Silva, and the words dried in his throat.

Da Silva was leaning back against the door, hips tilted provocatively forward. His eyes were hooded, black hair dishevelled, lips parted and a little red, like a man who had been thoroughly kissed. The silky dressing gown was open, revealing his smooth, bare chest and, Curtis couldn't but notice, dark nipples, one of which—oh, good God—was pierced with a silver ring.

He looked decadent beyond belief. He looked as though someone had been about to fuck him right there against the door, and as though he'd have liked it.

Someone, and it would be obvious to the servants who that was.

Curtis felt the blood flame in his cheeks and forced his gaze away, back to the guns.

"Put those down." He managed something like a note of command.

"Beg your pardon, gentlemen," said one of the older men woodenly, lowering his shotgun a fraction, so that he could not quite be said to be pointing it at a guest. Curtis wasn't reassured. "An alarm went off. Were you leaning on the door just now, at all, sir?"

"The door," da Silva repeated, mouth curling in that secret smile. "Ye-e-es, perhaps a trifle. That set an alarm off, did it?"

"Might have. If you was leaning very heavy-like. Sir."

"Or if someone else was—" began Wesley, smirking and allowing his gun to droop. The grizzled man made a low, warning noise. Wesley's grin vanished and he muttered, "Sorry, Mr. March," as his shotgun swung back up. Curtis wanted to order him to put it down at once. He was held back by the thought that he didn't know what he'd do if the man refused.

"Unfortunate accident," he said instead. He ought to help da Silva's brilliant, unspeakable improvisation somehow, but it was as much as he could do to get the words out, choking with embarrassment, the bare-chested man lounging in the corner of his vision. "Sorry for any trouble."

"Sir," March said flatly. "Excuse me." He strode towards the storeroom door as he spoke, lowering the shotgun but keeping himself ready, not bothering to apologise as da Silva was forced to shift out of his way. The other two men waited in position, weapons still raised.

March tried the door, checking it was locked, and looked up at the contacts with a frown. "It shouldn't have done that." He gave it a small push, then shoved harder. "Doesn't seem to be loose. Now, why would that have gone off?" He looked round at Curtis again, eyes assessing. "There's nobody else in here, is there, sir?"

"I'd suggest there's a generous sufficiency of people as it is." Da Silva sounded light and mocking, without a hint of shame or guilt. "An excess, even, so I shall remove myself at once. I do beg your pardon for, ah, arousing you from your beds." He gave Wesley the briefest flutter of his long lashes. "And I shall return to mine. Or someone's, anyway. Come, my dear." That was to Curtis, with a taunting smile.

March gave him a long look, which da Silva ignored, and nodded to his underlings. "Wesley, Preston, make sure the gentlemen find their way."

Da Silva tapped Curtis on the arm in summons and led the way along the corridor and to the main stairs, hips swaying outrageously. Curtis followed. He could feel March's suspicious look until he left the room, and the gaze of the others as they tracked him up the stairs, along the corridor, past the glass cases of dead hunting birds. The presence of the guns seemed almost physical behind his undefended back. The hairs on his neck were standing straight.

The servants stopped at the entrance to the east corridor, watching them as they headed down the dark passage in silence till they reached the two adjacent bedrooms. Curtis opened his own door and switched on the light.

Da Silva shoved him in, kicked the door shut with his heel, and launched into a low-voiced and uncomplimentary assessment of Curtis's intelligence, abilities, sexual tastes and parentage. For a poet, he had the vocabulary of a costermonger.

"I *know*," Curtis got in, when da Silva was forced to stop for breath. "I'm a damned fool. I forgot all about the alarm. That was jolly quick thinking of yours, we'd have been sunk otherwise."

"We're not watertight yet. Listen."

Curtis listened. There were very soft sounds of movement, but not from outside the door. The noise was coming from the other side of the opposite wall, the side with the mirror, the secret spy corridor. He heard a slight scrape.

"They've come to watch," da Silva said, voice low and tense. "I'm not sure March believed me. You're too bloody soldierly. *Shit.*"

Curtis set his jaw. He'd got them into this; he'd get them out. He kept his voice very quiet, turning away from the mirror so his lips couldn't be read. "If it comes to a scrap, I've my Webley in the wardrobe. Are you armed?"

"I don't use guns. You think you can fight our way out?"

Two armed men watching them and another waiting downstairs. His revolver packed away and unloaded. A thirty-mile night trek over rough unfamiliar terrain even if they got out of the house without pursuit. And da Silva was not the partner he'd have chosen for either fight or flight. "The odds aren't good," Curtis admitted. "But if it comes to that—"

"If it comes to that, we've lost. We might get away, but the evidence will be long gone." Da Silva hesitated. "Oh, hell. Get on the bed."

"What?"

Da Silva snaked an arm round his neck, gave him a provocative smile, hooked a foot round his ankle and shoved him backwards. Curtis stumbled, and sat heavily on the mattress.

There was a whisper of silk as da Silva shed his dressing gown and stood, naked to the waist. The little ring gleamed silver against his dark nipple.

"What the devil are you doing?"

"Smile, we're being watched." Da Silva sank to his knees and tugged Curtis's gown off his shoulders. "Just try to enjoy it, I'll do the work."

"Work?" said Curtis hoarsely. "What—?"

"If they decide we were faking, that you were at that bloody cabinet, we're probably dead." Da Silva ran his mouth up Curtis's neck, towards his ear. "So we're going to make it convincing, understand? Or"—he trailed a finger back down Curtis's chest—"you can sit there like a sack of potatoes till they decide you *weren't* poncing me in the library and come back with shotguns." He looked up, head tilted at a flirtatious angle. "Do you have any better ideas? Because I don't."

Curtis had no ideas at all, because da Silva's hands were on his waistband now. He made a choking noise in his throat.

"It's only a mouth. They're all the same," da Silva hissed. "Come on, you did this at school, didn't you? Pretend you're back at Eton."

"You can't do this!"

"What's your alternative?"

Curtis didn't have an alternative. Da Silva was kneeling before him, dark eyes snapping, that outrageous ring twinkling with the rise and fall of his chest, skilful hands hovering over Curtis's buttons and the hard swell of his groin.

"Well?"

Curtis shook his head, the smallest movement. He wasn't sure what he was refusing.

"Then lie back and think of England." Da Silva tugged at his trousers, and Curtis shifted up to allow him to pull away the fabric. He shut his eyes, felt da Silva's hands on the buttons of his drawers. Light fingers brushed the tip of his cock.

"Oh God."

"Relax," murmured da Silva. "I won't bite." And with that, Curtis was engulfed in warm, wet sensation.

His eyes sprang open, and he saw himself in that conveniently positioned mirror, face flushed, leaning back with his legs spread, and the dark man kneeling between his thighs, head bowed.

Someone was behind that mirror, watching.

"I can't," he hissed.

Da Silva made a noise of exasperation. "I'm doing the hard part. Just shut your eyes."

Curtis couldn't have shut his eyes on a bet. He was looking at the mirror, and he should have been thinking of what was happening on the other side of the wall, but he was transfixed by the contrast between the slender lines of da Silva's smooth olive-skinned back, and his own much paler chest, thickly furred with dark blond hair over the broad, powerful pectorals. And da Silva's mouth was on his stiff length, working hard, tongue dipping and curling and licking, and it was becoming impossible to think of anything else but that.

This was not the slobbery fumbling he remembered from school, or the awkward manoeuvring at college. Da Silva's cheeks, lightly scratchy with stubble, rasped against his thighs. His clever tongue ran over the head of Curtis's cock, pushing and nudging, then his mouth closed over him completely, and his lips slid down along the rigid length, taking him deep in his throat, all the way down.

Curtis made an animal noise. It was obscene, and astonishing, and he had no idea how da Silva wasn't choking. He leaned back, staring down at the dark head and—he had to make it look convincing, da Silva had said—reached for his hair, tentative at first, then running his hands through the brilliantined sleekness, feeling the movement of the man's head as his cheeks and throat worked. Da Silva rubbed the side of his face like a cat against the leather of Curtis's glove. His throat vibrated with a soft purr that hummed against Curtis's flesh and sang through his blood. Curtis bit his lip.

Make it convincing. His hips were moving now, almost without his volition, pushing himself into da Silva's clever, pretty, filthy mouth. Da Silva's fingers were running over his flanks, and his mouth worked impossibly, clenching and

69

sucking, up and down, and Curtis forgot the watchers, and Lafayette, and everything else. He felt nothing but the hot mouth on him, saw nothing but the mirrored form of a dark angel between his legs. He drove harder, gripping the man's hair to keep him close, and da Silva moaned with what sounded like pleasure, fingers digging into his thighs to pull him on, taking the thrusts without recoiling. God, he actually liked it, he liked having Curtis's big, engorged prick in his mouth...

Curtis felt his balls tighten painfully, far too soon, and dimly remembered his manners. "Going to come," he warned hoarsely.

Da Silva dragged his lips upwards, away, and Curtis had a second to regret his own chivalry before the other man plunged down again, taking his whole length in a single smooth movement, sending waves of sensation crashing across his skin.

"Christ, da Silva, stop, I'll come in your mouth!"

Da Silva grunted, sucking even harder, and did that thing with his throat again, muscles rippling and clutching, and Curtis came with a stifled shout, gripping da Silva's head hard, not caring if he choked him, hips jerking frantically as he spent in jet after fierce jet.

He released his grip on da Silva's hair, feeling the oil on the bare skin of his left hand, and flopped back, stunned. At his crotch, he heard the kneeling man swallow.

Curtis stared up at the ceiling.

Da Silva stood and moved to pour himself a glass of water from the nightstand, sloshing it around his mouth.

The bed creaked as da Silva came and sat on it, not touching. "All right?"

Curtis had no idea if he was all right. He looked over at da Silva. His dark hair was tousled and tangled, falling forward, so that he no longer looked sleek and self-possessed, but rougher, more real, loosened by intimacy. His lips were swollen with pressure, or arousal. The silver ring glinted against a nipple that was tight and erect.

Did he want Curtis to reciprocate?

"You look like you're about to have a heart attack," da Silva remarked. "I'm not sure whether I should find that flattering or the opposite."

Their situation crashed down on Curtis then, driving out the madness of the last few minutes. "Dear God," he hissed. "Don't you understand—they'll have bloody photographed that!" He sat up as he spoke, grabbing for his dressing gown, suddenly desperate to cover himself.

"No, will they?" Da Silva rolled his eyes. "That was the *point*."

Curtis spluttered. "We could both be arrested!"

"Better than dead. Don't panic, for heaven's sake. We were playing cock in cover in the library, we had no idea they would photograph that interlude, therefore we don't know what they're up to, *therefore* it was a false alarm. We're out of the woods, as long as you don't raise anyone's suspicions by having a conniption now." He gave Curtis a slanted, not quite real smile. "No need to thank me."

Curtis couldn't believe he'd said that. "And what if they use the photographs? Hand them to the police?" Christ almighty. Five minutes of da Silva's mouth and he was looking at two years for gross indecency.

"They're blackmailers, you idiot, they don't call the police. I have to get the films back, that's all." Da Silva sounded infuriatingly unruffled. "Calm down. This is trivial."

"*Trivial?* You might not care about being caught in some ghastly compromising situation—"

Da Silva's face tightened. "I care less about that than about being caught with my hands in our host's till. Which, let me remind you, was what you brought on us when you blundered straight through that wire."

"I know that, damn it!"

"Keep your voice down," da Silva hissed. "And have you a better idea of how I could have deflected suspicion away from your stupidity, before you rant at me for sullying your inviolate body with my dirty ways?"

Curtis was sure he hadn't said that, and didn't much appreciate da Silva putting words in his mouth, but he was in no state to conduct an argument on two flanks. "Well, how the hell are we better off now?"

"We haven't been knocked on the head and buried under the redwoods?"

"I might as bloody well be!" Curtis had to fight to keep his voice to a whisper. "*You* might be used to posing for filthy photographs—"

"Yes, poor you, it must have been awful." Da Silva's low tone rang with icy fury. "You're a martyr to your country. You underrate your skills at dissembling, though, I could have sworn you were able to endure the disgusting business without too much agony." He gave Curtis a vicious fake smile. "After all, you came."

That was just bloody rude, and Curtis found himself retorting, "You made me come!"

Even as he realised how childish that sounded, da Silva was on his feet. "Well, I beg your pardon for imposing myself on you. Next time you may pick your own locks, solve your own problems, and suck your own cock. Good night, Mr. Curtis."

He stalked out. Curtis stared after him.

After a few moments sitting on the bed, looking at nothing, he readied himself for sleep with automatic movements. He tried not to look into the mirror, not to think, not to hear any noises from across the hall—of course there weren't any, this was da Silva.

He turned off the light and lay in bed, looking at the dark.

He'd had to do it, of course. There was no question about what they had found, or the Armstrongs' ruthlessness in keeping their secrets. Armstrong's men had been watching, suspicious. He—they—had had to do *something*. Curtis wouldn't have thought of da Silva's solution in a hundred years, but since he hadn't come up with an alternative then or now, he could hardly complain.

He couldn't pretend it had been a hardship, of course. Granted, he'd enjoyed it, but who wouldn't? Any man would have felt the same pleasure, he was sure of that. Anyone would have come under those astonishing ministrations, that tight, hot throat, the exploring tongue. Especially a man who had been bereft of companionship for so long. A fellow had needs, and da Silva certainly knew how to satisfy them.

He was sure da Silva had taken pleasure in sucking him too. Those sounds he'd made, the purr in his throat, the little moan... Did that change things? Make it, well, queer?

Surely not. It could make no difference to Curtis whether da Silva had enjoyed the act or not. And the fellow might be a pansy but he seemed a decent sort of chap at heart, underneath the mannerisms and the hard, prickly shell. Curtis wouldn't have wanted him to find the act disgusting.

It would have been a great deal worse if da Silva *wasn't* a queer sort, now he considered it. What then? What if Curtis had had to kneel in front of da Silva, to take him in his mouth...

His mind was wandering. He needed to sleep.

He'd had too many disturbed nights here to stay wakeful for long, and the years of campaigning had taught him to empty his mind, no matter his daylight concerns. As he drifted off, the one thought that stayed with him wasn't the cabinet's contents, or the later events. It was that caressing, intimate rub of da Silva's face against his leather glove.

Chapter Six

The next morning, it rained.

Curtis sat at the breakfast table with his fellow guests. Da Silva, who seemed to be an unrepentantly late riser, was not among them. He was glad of that. He needed to speak to him, of course. They needed to work out how to bring their information to whoever might listen and act, and Curtis knew he should get things back on an even keel after last night's drama, but he wasn't sorry to put it off a little longer. Coming in a chap's mouth made it rather awkward to look him in the eye.

It was bad enough making polite conversation with the Armstrongs.

The servants would have told their masters about last night, he was sure. One or the other Armstrong, maybe all three, would know what he'd done with da Silva. That was not a comfortable thought. Of course, the Armstrongs would not let on that they knew—if they said anything, it would be as the opening to extortion, and Curtis had resolved to deal with that promptly and forcefully. It would be something of a relief. But if the Armstrongs were keeping up the facade of normality, even the most compliant host might object to his guests setting off alarms with indecent, illegal behaviour in the library, and if Sir Hubert decided to have a quiet word of rebuke, Curtis would have to endure it, apologise even.

He had spared da Silva a few unkind thoughts as he came down to breakfast, braced for humiliation, but so far it appeared that the country-house rules of pretended ignorance applied. Sir Hubert was genial, Lady Armstrong wonderfully lively, rippling with laughter as she made mock lamentations about the rain. Lambdon and James Armstrong spoke like decent English fellows.

They were all so pleasant that last night took on even more of a dreamlike quality as he ate. He couldn't reconcile these companionable, civilised people with the foul cabinet and its sheaves of betrayal, treachery and death. He could hardly believe anything of the events of last night, except that his black leather glove was still shiny where he had gripped da Silva's brilliantined hair.

Da Silva drifted in halfway through the meal. His deep-set eyes were ringed with dark circles of sleeplessness, but he was impeccably dressed, hair sleeked back. Curtis wished he wouldn't wear the stuff. He had a momentary mental image of da Silva's tumbled locks last night, and blinked it away.

He gave an awkward nod of greeting and received a blank look.

"I was just saying to everyone, Mr. da Silva," said Lady Armstrong in her silvery tones, "if it clears up this afternoon, I propose a walk to the limestone caves. They're just a couple of miles away and so dramatic, I feel sure you'd be inspired."

"I must decline. I abominate the subterranean, and my editorial labours call me. Do enjoy your explorations." Da Silva helped himself to a kipper, apparently unaware that one should not contradict a lady, let alone one's hostess. Curtis had to give him credit for sheer effrontery. The other men exchanged "what can you expect?" glances.

"In the meantime, do please resort to the games room," Lady Armstrong went on. "Cards, billiards, and perhaps, if the weather sets in badly, we could plan a round of charades?"

"Oh, wonderful," said Miss Carruth with enthusiasm. "I adore charades."

Curtis couldn't help glancing at da Silva. He was eating the smoked fish with catlike delicacy, a man with nothing more in his mind than avoiding pin bones.

Charades, indeed.

After breakfast Curtis, Grayling and Holt repaired to the billiard room, somehow bringing da Silva in their wake. James Armstrong and Lambdon had gone off with Miss Carruth and Mrs. Grayling, both ladies giggling with flirtatious amusement. Lady Armstrong had watched them with a smile that had seemed to Curtis just a little fixed.

"Do you play, da Silva?" Holt asked sceptically.

Da Silva didn't react to the tone. "Less than I used to. I remember the principles."

"Who's playing who?" asked Holt.

"I'll give you a game," said Grayling with obvious haste to avoid being partnered with the wrong man. Da Silva's mouth curled.

Curtis said, "Then it's you and I, da Silva."

"Can you play with that?" Da Silva nodded at his hand as Curtis chalked his cue.

"I've had plenty of practice. Don't worry, you won't be at an advantage." He made a good break and straightened, pleased.

"I wouldn't be too sure of that," da Silva said, and proceeded to pot the next two balls.

Curtis stood back, moving from surprise to respect as da Silva worked the table. His hands were as deft on the cue as on the lockpicks, and he was obviously assessing the whole game as he moved round the table with economic grace, setting up the next shot each time he struck a ball. Curtis, a decent enough player but no strategist, watched with frank admiration.

Da Silva leaned over for a tricky shot. A lock of black hair fell loose, and he shook it away with a toss of his head. They had all stripped to waistcoats and shirtsleeves, and his cuffs were rolled back to reveal brown forearms. He was bent forward over the table, the position pulling his clothing tight over his slender, elegant body, those close-fitting trousers outlining a taut, very well-shaped backside. His lips were slightly parted in concentration, and Curtis had a sudden, powerful image of himself taking hold of the dark head as he lay sprawled on the table, of pushing his cock into that inviting mouth—

Curtis heard the hitch in his own breathing. Da Silva's head jerked up as he struck, and his shot cannoned off the cushions.

"Blast. Your table, Curtis."

He sounded nothing more than a touch annoyed at himself. Curtis nodded dumbly, fouled his next shot, and lost the game by a wide and deserved margin.

"Yes, well, very good." Holt was looking over at them. "How are you against a fellow with two hands?"

"Still very good." Da Silva's smile glittered.

"Is that right. Would you care to put a wager on it?"

"No."

"Not that confident?"

"On the contrary."

"I'll back da Silva, if we're placing wagers," Curtis offered, trying to keep the atmosphere pleasant. "I don't think I've ever been so trounced."

"A quid says otherwise." Holt looked at da Silva with an unmistakable sneer. "Not backing yourself? Of course, you people are careful with the pennies."

Da Silva's eyes hooded, but the smile stayed on his lips. "Increase your stake, Curtis. I have your honour to uphold."

"I shouldn't." Grayling looked uncomfortable. "Holt's awfully good."

Holt gave a modest shrug. "I can hold my own."

"I dare say you have to," murmured da Silva.

"I'll make it a fiver," Curtis put in, before anyone else thought twice about that remark.

"You're a high flyer. It's a shame to take your money. Here." Holt handed a coin to da Silva to toss for first strike. "Don't 'forget' to give it back."

Da Silva, who had been about to flip the coin, took it between finger and thumb and dropped it onto the baize of the table. "You go first."

Holt gave him a hostile look, then picked up the coin. Da Silva smiled. "Buy me a drink from your winnings, Curtis."

"Really, what side," muttered Grayling.

Holt was a good player, Curtis had seen that earlier. The two men seemed evenly matched at first. Holt took a serious approach to the game, with frowning concentration. Da Silva did nothing to break it—one couldn't have accused him of the slightest failure of sportsmanship—but his affected stance while Holt worked, hand on hip, head tilted, could have been calculated to annoy any red-blooded man. In fact, Curtis realised, it probably was.

With the table half-cleared, the clock chimed. Da Silva, about to strike the ball, gave a breathy gasp and straightened, lifting his cue dramatically. "Was that the half-hour? Good heavens, time does fly in such charming company. I've *so* much work to do, you know. The Muse demands sacrifice."

"You're not abandoning the game?" Holt demanded.

"Heavens, no, not at all. But I *can't* dally any longer." Da Silva chalked his cue again, bent back to the table and proceeded to clear it without missing a shot.

The Englishmen watched open-mouthed. Da Silva moved like a snake, sinuous, unhesitating and absurdly fast, bringing his cue to each ball without waiting to see if the previous one had dropped into a pocket. The silence in the room was absolute except for Holt's stertorous breathing, the whisper of ball on baize, and the click of ivory meeting ivory.

The last ball spun into its pocket, and da Silva straightened. "There," he told Holt. "All done. Don't 'forget' to pay Curtis, will you?"

He slotted his cue back into the rack, donned his coat with great care, adjusted his cuffs and strolled out.

"Well, I say," said Grayling into the silence. "Honestly."

"I knew it." Holt was scarlet. "The man's nothing more than a sharp."

"Nonsense," Curtis said.

"Nonsense? Did you see that?"

"He was toying with Holt," said Grayling, undiplomatically. "Could have thrashed him any time he wanted."

Holt glared at him. "A sharp, I tell you. They play like that in Jew-boy billiard halls in the East End—"

Curtis cut in. "They may do, but you can't accuse a man of sharping you when he refused to play for money."

"I don't see why the devil you're taking his side." Holt looked startled and a little hurt by Curtis's defection. Curtis felt somewhat startled himself, but a fact was a fact.

"He beat you fair and square, and not for money either. He's a damned good player, which leaves the rest of us to be good losers." Curtis let that sink in; a poor loser was a much-despised creature. Holt pressed his lips together. "Now, do you want to try and win back some of that fiver you owe me?"

They played two more games, and Curtis lost a fair amount of his notional winnings. It smoothed Holt's ruffled feathers somewhat, but he still seemed aggrieved. Curtis couldn't blame him.

He couldn't really blame da Silva either. Holt hadn't said anything much out of the ordinary, and one might have thought da Silva would be used to that sort of banter. He would hear it often enough, after all. But Curtis had fought the Boers, a handful of ill-equipped farmers who had almost defeated the British Empire through sheer obstinate pride, and he had recognised the flash in da Silva's dark liquid eyes. A Latin tag that he'd learned as a schoolboy came to mind, along with its doggerel translation. *Nemo me impune lacessit. If you cross me, you'll regret it.*

He went off to seek the subject of his thoughts and succeeded on the first try: the library, where Misses Merton and Carruth were exploring the shelves. Da Silva sat at the desk, hair slicked back into place, intent on his work.

Curtis came up, aware of the women. "Good game. You're a fine player."

"Years of practice." Da Silva didn't look up. He had two dictionaries and a pile of manuscript sheets in front of him, which he seemed to be annotating. Curtis came over to look. The original handwriting was execrable; da Silva's additions were in a looping, elaborate hand and, regrettably, maroon ink. Curtis squinted to read them upside down.

"Editing Levy is not a spectator sport." Da Silva's pen scratched. He didn't seem inclined to pay Curtis any attention.

"Who's Levy?"

"The leading Fragmentalist. One of England's greatest living poets." Da Silva contemplated the word he'd written, crossed it out again, and added, "If you mention Alfred Austin, I shall strike you."

"Mr. da Silva!" Fenella Carruth giggled. "Mr. Austin *is* the Poet Laureate."

"Which demonstrates the artistic void of that appalling institution." As da Silva, spoke, he wrote in clear print, on the paper, and the right way up for Curtis to read, *Folly—1hr.* The pen tapped the words to call Curtis's attention, paused for just a few seconds and then scratched the message out. "Kindly leave me to my labours. I find the military stance unconducive to the pursuit of the Muse."

"Sorry to interrupt you," murmured Curtis, exchanging glances with Miss Merton, and went to see if the house would supply him with oilskins.

Chapter Seven

He arrived at the folly somewhat damp after a lengthy but refreshing tramp in the rain. His leg wasn't paining him as much as usual. The doctors had long insisted that the kneecap had suffered no grave damage, and seemed to think he should have made a full recovery by now. Curtis had not let himself believe it, then or more recently. The wounds of Jacobsdal weren't the kind that healed. But as he approached the ridiculous medieval tower on the brow of the hill, he was not thinking about the pain, or the blood on dry earth that it brought back, but about the ugly truths that lay under Peakholme's smooth facade like the thing in da Silva's fishponds, and the dark, slender man he was going to meet.

He let himself into the folly and shook the wet off his borrowed oilskins.

"Up here," came a voice from above, making Curtis rear back like a startled horse. "Bar the door."

Curtis dumped the oilskins on a chest, dropped the heavy oak bar into place in its big iron holders—one couldn't fault Sir Hubert or his architect's attention to detail there, the thick door would hold a small army out—and rounded the stairs. The mezzanine floor took up about half the breadth of the round tower, its thick oak warmer on the feet than the flagstones of the ground floor. Da Silva stood, away from the windows, shoulders propped against the wall and arms folded. He had his large fur-collared overcoat draped around his shoulders.

"It's quite warm in here," Curtis observed, shedding his own overcoat. "Solid construction."

"One would hardly want a ruin to be inhospitable, would one? We should speak of last night."

Curtis swallowed. "Yes."

"Blackmail and treason. We need to get our information to the proper authorities without anyone here twigging what we're up to, and we need to remove any evidence of last night's efforts at alleviating suspicion."

Alleviating suspicion, Curtis thought. Da Silva's hot mouth, sliding up and down his length, the clever tongue curling round the head of his cock, the nipple ring that had pressed briefly against Curtis's bare thigh when da Silva had leaned against him. "Yes."

"Like you, I accepted an invitation for a fortnight." Da Silva spoke with his usual smoothness. If he was feeling the flood of sensory memory that was assailing Curtis, it didn't show in his face. Had he sucked off so many men that one more left him unmoved? "I'd rather not wait that long before raising the alarm. Either of us might give our knowledge away at any time."

"You mean that I might, I suppose."

Da Silva shrugged. "However, I'm not sure how we go about calling for help. The house telephone goes through an exchange located here, via an operator, who is a servant of the Armstrongs and Peakholme."

"They'll listen in, you think?"

"I'm quite sure they will. It *might* be all right to send a telegram or a letter, but I wouldn't put it past them to open their guests' post, and I am sure that they'd open yours and mine, in the hope of written admissions, or even other names to pursue."

"I expect they might. Well then, one or the other of us will have to cut our visit short."

"It's the best option. It would be terribly rude to our hosts, of course."

"I'm sure you could manage that," Curtis said.

A glimmer of amusement lit da Silva's eyes. "Doubtless." He hesitated. "Not to embarrass you, but we should address the question of any compromising photographs that may have been taken last night. I think we have to assume they *were* taken."

Curtis nodded. He could imagine what the damned things looked like as if he held them in his hands. His thickly muscled bare chest, his face contorted with pleasure, the slim dark man kneeling between his thighs, head bowed.

"The problem is not just finding the films, and any photographs made from them. It's that removing them makes it obvious that we know what the Armstrongs are up to. Then either they will have to deal with us, or they will destroy the evidence in that cabinet, or both." Da Silva removed his heavy overcoat and laid it down with care. "It is warm, isn't it. What I would prefer is to take the evidence of all the illegal activity, ours and theirs, and depart without ceremony. Did you motor here?"

"Can't," Curtis managed. How could he talk so casually? "My hand. I can't grip the wheel. Can you drive?"

"No. We could, I suppose, walk, but I don't imagine you like the idea of a thirty-mile tramp across rough terrain in this weather any more than I do, and Armstrong's men will doubtless move faster and know the country better."

"The ground's too open for that, if you're worried about pursuit." This at least was familiar stuff. "Very little cover, long lines of sight. Have you any experience with stalking?" The slender, velvet-coated form lounging against the wall did not seem to belong to a man used to open spaces.

Da Silva shuddered. "God, no. I don't hunt. Very well, we've no means of a quick exit. I think, then, you should return to London for a chat with your Uncle Maurice. This is his sort of business. Warn me by telegram—I'll give you some innocuous wording to use—and I will remove those pictures before the troops get here."

Curtis frowned at that. It was casually put, but what it came down to was da Silva alone, risking discovery by dangerous men. "Why don't you go to London and I'll stay?"

"You can't pick locks."

"You can't deal with the alarm."

"I watched you. It was hardly a complicated process. You could teach me."

Curtis probably could, but that was still unacceptable. "I think the risk of attack from the Armstrongs is far greater for you than for me." He didn't need to spell out why. If something happened to well-born, wealthy war hero Archie Curtis, important people would care. The redoubtable Sir Maurice Vaizey and the old warrior Sir Henry Curtis would not rest till they had found their nephew, alive or dead. Da Silva had no birth or social standing, he was unlikely to have influential friends, and the Armstrongs would not expect the disappearance of a *demimonde* Portuguese Jew to cause concern in any circles that mattered. Curtis would make one hell of a fuss if anything happened to the man, of course, but by then it would be too late.

Da Silva was shaking his head. "I wouldn't be so sure. I think you may underestimate the ruthlessness at play here, and if you'll forgive the plain speaking, you are not well equipped to deal with that."

Curtis stared at him, almost speechless. How dare the bloody effeminate say—how dare he imply—? He took a very deep breath. "I can look after myself, and a damned sight better than some prancing pansy. *You* take this information out. Talking's what you're good at."

"Oh dear God, the British soldier, heroically setting his jaw against overwhelming odds. You don't have a Gatling gun here." Da Silva's tone was caustic.

"I'm not afraid of the bloody Armstrongs."

"This is not about fighting. This is about evidence, and how we transfer it from them to us, so that at the end of this farrago, they are arrested and we are not. If the Armstrongs destroy everything in that cabinet before the authorities see it, we'll have failed. If they use those damned photographs against us, you'll be looking at a scandal at best, two years hard at worst."

"And if the Armstrongs or those men of theirs catch you sneaking around?" Curtis demanded. "What about that shallow grave under the redwoods?"

Da Silva winced. "I shall attempt to avoid that. This isn't worth the argument. Just go to London and leave the rest to me."

"The devil I will." Curtis took a furious stride forward. "If you think I'm coward enough to hide behind your skirts—"

"I beg your pardon?"

"I will not protect my honour at the risk of another man's life," Curtis gritted out. "That is not what honour means. Do you understand that?"

"In fact, despite being a mere dago, I understand very well what honour means." Da Silva looked rather white around the mouth. "I forced you into that encounter last night. I'll deal with the consequences."

"I'm not a bloody woman and I don't need your bloody protection from a compromising situation, like some tart in a melodrama!" Curtis glared into his face. "Who the hell do you think you are to give me orders?"

"Dear sweet heaven. This is not the moment to reclaim your masculinity."

"*What?*"

He was right up against da Silva now. The slighter man had his back to the wall, and there was alarm in his dark eyes, but no sign of retreat.

"I'm sorry I infringed your manliness last night," da Silva bit out. "I apologise for sucking your cock. I realise you would prefer to act the noble hero after such an unmanning experience, but *I* am more concerned with getting the Armstrongs to the gallows without either of us suffering in the process. Understand?"

Curtis was choking on everything he wanted to say. Angry denial jostled with the desire to put the bloody encroaching sod in his place, to stop him talking. And worst of all was the awareness sparked by da Silva's crude, shameless words. He wanted to hit him. He wanted to grab him and drag him forward, as da Silva had seized him back in the library last night. He had no idea what he'd do when he got hold of him.

"I *apologise*," da Silva hissed, sounding more like a Cape cobra than a man expressing regret. "I abase myself, I grovel, is that what you need to hear? Would it help if I fell to my knees?"

Curtis's heart stopped. The image in his mind was all-consuming. He couldn't speak, and he knew his face must be betraying him but he couldn't seem to control it. There was a tiny, ringing moment of silence.

"Ah," said da Silva.

Curtis couldn't quite breathe through the tightness in his chest. Da Silva's eyes were unreadable, and his lips were parted, and very close.

"Is that it? If I went to my knees, is that what you want?"

This was outrageous. Unjustifiable. No excuse now. Curtis was as stiff and hard as a gun barrel, and he was quite sure that da Silva knew it.

Da Silva straightened away from the wall so that he was no more than a few inches from Curtis's face, his body a whisper away. "Conditions, Curtis. If I do this, it is because you want it. You ask me for it. You do not accuse me of forcing anything on you against your will."

Curtis made an inarticulate noise of protest at the very idea. Da Silva's eyes were dark on his. "I mean it. If it would salve your bruised manliness to have your cock sucked, then say so."

Curtis had no idea why da Silva was accusing him of feeling unmanly. He hadn't felt so masculine in years. Desire was another thing Jacobsdal had taken from him, along with fingers and career and friends; he had barely summoned up the energy for the relief of his left hand in months. Now, as he stared at those parted lips, knowing what they could do, he felt as though da Silva had blown up a dam and set a torrent thundering through a long-dry course.

But he wasn't a poet, so he didn't say that.

"Tell me what you want." Da Silva's voice was tight, breathing hard.

"I want...I want you to do it."

"Do *what*?"

"On your knees," Curtis said. "Suck me."

Da Silva whisked a handkerchief from his pocket and spread it on the floorboards, kneeling on it. Curtis watched his movements, frozen with incredulity and need. Then da Silva, without looking up, took hold of his waistband. Buttons flicked, cloth was pushed aside, and his rigid cock was out, achingly hard. It looked huge next to da Silva's handsome features.

"What do you want? Do you want to come in my mouth?"

"Oh God, yes. Please."

"Courtesy is always welcome," murmured da Silva, and took him in his lips.

Curtis gazed down, watching his thick member sliding in and out of da Silva's mouth as if it belonged to someone else. Da Silva's tongue and throat worked around him, and his hands came up to cup Curtis's rear, and even through cloth that was extraordinary, to be touched so. He began to move a little, in time with da Silva's movements, and felt the fingers tighten, and then one hand moved inside his drawers and da Silva was cupping his balls, and then—oh dear God—there was a finger sliding over his backside, along the crease.

"No," said Curtis hoarsely, because the sensation was too much, too intimate, but as da Silva snatched his touch away, he wished he hadn't spoken.

Da Silva pulled his head back and off, so that Curtis could see the full length of his own engorged cock, glistening with saliva. "I beg your pardon. Why don't you fuck my mouth, then?"

He gripped the head of Curtis's cock again, between his lips, and Curtis did it, he thrust hard, into da Silva's throat, taking hold of his head, pushing in. He heard the noises the man made, high-pitched whimpers, as both hands grabbed his straining buttocks, and he wondered vaguely if da Silva was going to come too, but there was no space in his mind for anything other than the ecstasy of Daniel da Silva's mouth around him now, and he thrust and thrust again, and came without warning or mercy in jets of hot pleasure down the poet's throat.

He let go of da Silva's hair after a few seconds, feeling his legs weak under him. Da Silva sat back on his heels, head down, the black locks tumbled.

Hands shaking, Curtis tucked himself away. His now-limp cock was almost agonisingly sensitive.

Da Silva knelt on the floor. He didn't move, or speak, or look at Curtis.

Curtis wanted to say something. Thank him. Touch him, even, because he remembered the school phrase, *turnabout is fair play*, and that was twice in twelve hours that da Silva had taken him to heaven. He wondered if da Silva was the same olive tint all over, and what exactly it was they cut off circumcised men.

Da Silva, still and silent, did not look receptive to being touched. Curtis extended a tentative hand, as if to an unfamiliar dog that might bite. There was no response.

"Da Silva? What about you?"

"What about me?" The vicious edge was back in his tone, and Curtis's warm pleasure at the contact drained away. He let his extended hand drop.

"Why did you do that?"

"*You* did it." Da Silva's head was still down. "Don't pretend that was all me."

"That's not what I meant." Did the fellow think he was some sort of hypocrite? "I meant— Are you all right?"

Da Silva did look up then.

"Absolutely. Marvellous. There is *nothing* I like more than a good fuck with someone who despises me."

That plunged Curtis into waters so uncharted that he wasn't sure which way was the surface and which the seabed. "What? I don't despise you."

"Don't you." Da Silva got up, brushing his trouser legs.

"I don't. That's nonsense."

"You called me a prancing pansy shortly before you shoved your cock in my mouth." He ran his fingers along the side of his jaw. "You should be careful with that thing, you could do damage."

Curtis felt a stab of guilt. "I didn't hurt you, did I?"

"No. It scarcely matters."

"Of course it matters. Wait, for God's sake." He seized da Silva's arm as he moved to take his coat. "*Wait.* Please. That was damned rude of me. I apologise. I—well, I resent not being the man I was."

"I gathered as much. Did we not just try to alleviate that?"

"I didn't mean that. Look, you're clearly a brave man, and you've put yourself in considerable danger to catch up with a blackmailer. But I've been in far worse situations than this, and I'm still better equipped to deal with devilry than you. The plain fact is, I'm a soldier, and you're a—"

"Queer?" sniped da Silva.

"Poet," said Curtis. "And that means *I* will take the physical risks here. I am not leaving you to face danger while I scurry off back to London. I don't appreciate the suggestion that I'm incapable, and I can't say I liked your manner of expressing yourself earlier. But I shouldn't have been so offensive in return, and I beg your pardon."

Curtis might as well have been speaking Swahili, for all the comprehension on da Silva's face. He looked bewildered. Curtis had no idea why, it seemed plain enough. He set his shoulders and went on, because it had to be said: "And I wish you'd tell me if I've done something wrong with—" He made a vague gesture, intended to encompass his groin and da Silva's mouth. "I may not have behaved as one should in these matters. I don't quite understand this sort of thing."

Da Silva opened his mouth, shut it again, and at last said, "No. You don't, and apparently, nor do I."

"I beg your pardon?"

"Just let me be sure I have this right. *That* was what you were angry about? Being edged out of the action? I gathered that your pride was at stake—"

Curtis knew he owed the fellow honesty. "I'm half-crippled. I don't need reminding of that. I don't find it easy to live with, and I don't like reminders that I'm less than I was."

"Well, God knows what you used to be, then, because you're built like a brick shithouse and hung like a horse."

Curtis blinked at that startling vulgarity. Da Silva gave him a wry half-smile. "But far be it from me to comment. Just tell me, are you, or were you, angry with me because I forced myself on you last night?"

Curtis groped for an answer and settled on, "No."

"Ri-i-ight." Da Silva drew the sound out.

"No," Curtis repeated. "Well, if I was angry, why would I have wanted you to do it again? It was, er, very decent of you," he added, feeling his cheeks redden.

Da Silva began to massage the bridge of his nose, as if staving off a headache. "Mmm. You're actually quite a straightforward sort of fellow, aren't you? I assumed—well, more fool me. I see. I do, in fact, see."

"See what?"

"What's in front of my face. With all that entails." Da Silva exhaled heavily. "Well. To begin with, I had no intention of questioning your physical abilities. I'm in no position to do that, and more to the point, I doubt violence will be useful here. Deception is what's required, and that's my area, not yours, which brings me to my second point. Quite frankly, not to beat about the bush, the reason I feel more qualified to handle this business than you—ah, this is embarrassing. I wasn't planning to tell you this."

"Tell me what?"

"Well, the thing is, when I implied—or said, really—that I was carrying out an amateur investigation, that wasn't quite accurate. I'm here professionally."

"Professionally? To do what, write sonnets?"

"No, my other profession." Da Silva looked as close to shamefaced as Curtis could imagine. "I work for the Foreign Office Private Bureau. For your Uncle Maurice, in fact. As one of his, er, special recruits."

The words made sense, but the meaning did not. "You work for the Private Bureau?" Curtis repeated.

"As I said."

"You're a secret agent?"

"I loathe that term. It's so violent, somehow."

"*You?*"

Da Silva rolled his eyes. "I suppose I should find your incredulity flattering. It would be lowering to learn I looked like a tool of the State."

"But— Why didn't you say?"

"*Secret* agent. Secret."

Curtis gaped, trying to imagine his uncompromisingly strict uncle recruiting this willowy decadent, then was hit by an abrupt, horrifying thought.

It was a pose. It was all a bloody pose. Da Silva was a government agent, deflecting suspicion with this brilliant, outrageous facade. He had sucked Curtis off last night for no more reason than to ensure they could bring home the information they needed, and today he, Curtis, he had—

He had forced the man to his knees and done that to him, used his mouth, not because da Silva wanted it, but because *he* did.

Curtis stared at him, appalled.

"Are you all right?" Da Silva's voice seemed to come from a long way away. "Curtis?"

"Oh dear God," Curtis mumbled, overwhelmed by shame. "I'm so sorry. Christ. I—I can't apologise enough."

"For...?"

This was intolerable, and he deserved every bit of it. "You must think I need horsewhipping."

"I really don't think that's what you need. What are you agonising about?"

"Good God, man, I just made you—" Curtis gestured at the floor where da Silva had knelt. "That. *I* made you. It was all my fault. I'm so sorry."

Da Silva looked down, then up, a peculiar expression on his face. "Is this flood of remorse because you've concluded I'm a government agent masquerading as a shameless invert?"

Curtis made himself meet his eyes. "I can only apologise. I had no idea."

"Dear fellow, you've missed it by a mile." Da Silva patted his arm comfortingly. "I'm a government agent *and* a shameless invert. Which is not to say I'll suck you off on demand, but if you think you've been ravaging my virgin mouth, you're about fifteen years and quite a lot of pricks too late."

"Oh, thank God," Curtis blurted out on a wave of sheer relief, and da Silva's composure cracked. He doubled over with laughter. Curtis shot him a furious look. "It's not bloody funny!"

"Yes, it is." Da Silva's eyes brimmed with amusement. His lips were reddened, hair dishevelled, and he looked so unbearably handsome it made Curtis's chest tighten.

He sat on the floor and put his head in his hands.

Da Silva made a good effort to regain control, though his voice was shaky as he said, "Come on, it's not that bad."

Curtis didn't reply. There was a short silence.

"Curtis?"

He couldn't do this, couldn't face it. How the hell did da Silva do it? How could he look him, anyone in the eye? Oh dear God, the man reported to his uncle.

"It *is* that bad. I see. Ah, if you're thinking of assaulting me, for God's sake *not* the face, but can I just point out that we still need to work together—"

"What are you babbling about?"

"I'm hoping you're not planning to hit me."

Curtis lifted his head at that. "Of course I'm not!"

"Delighted to hear it." Da Silva dropped to squat next to him with a whisper of movement. "I abhor violence, particularly when it's directed at me."

"Why on earth would I do any such thing?" Curtis found himself ruffled by the suggestion. He might not be an intellectual, but he wasn't a bloody brute.

"Oh, well. Some men appear to feel that it's less queer to have a chap suck one's cock if one abuses him afterwards."

"Well, I don't," Curtis said, and then realised that didn't sound quite right. "Hit chaps for doing that, I mean. Not that it comes up, of course—" Da Silva clamped his lips together, looking very like he was trying not to laugh again. Curtis glared at him. "What I mean is, obviously it *doesn't* make one queer, having a fellow do that for one. I'm not your sort."

"Of course not."

"Well, I'm not. I just—that was... It's not the same thing, is it?"

"Nothing like it," da Silva agreed obligingly.

"That's not the point, anyway," said Curtis, dragging the conversation back from this unnecessary tangent. "The point is, that business just now was my fault, so I am certainly not going to blame you for it."

"I appreciate the sentiment, but fault doesn't come into it." Da Silva pulled out his pocket watch. "We should be getting back to the house, it'll be luncheon soon. Will you listen to me a moment?"

"I seem to do nothing but listen to you," Curtis said with feeling. "You could jaw the hind leg off a donkey."

"A beast to which you bear a striking resemblance, in more than one way." The twitch of da Silva's brow robbed the little jab of any sting. "Firstly, I will retrieve these photographs, because I am better placed to do it than you. End of discussion. Secondly, I hope you won't indulge in any regrets over this encounter. Chalk it up to a misunderstanding, a sleepless night and a dramatic situation. Consider it forgotten."

That sounded like something he should be relieved to hear. Da Silva didn't give him pause to think.

"Thirdly, and this is the important one: dead men. Dead men under the sun of Jacobsdal or floating down the Thames at night. Dead and smashed in the seas off Beachy Head, or in lonely rooms with a gun falling from their hands, or in the next war because of the secrets that have been sold. The Armstrongs have left a trail of blood for their own enrichment, and I intend to bring them to justice. And I am quite sure that you will stand with me to do it, whatever else happens, because if you are a man to put personal concerns before duty, then I have lost my judgement."

Curtis inhaled deeply, taking on the words without excuses. "I beg your pardon, da Silva. You won't need to remind me again."

Da Silva nodded, as one professional to another. He stood, and extended a hand to pull Curtis up. Curtis, who outweighed him by several stone of muscle, took it, feeling da Silva's fingers warm around his for a moment.

"Very well," da Silva said. "I'll slip out first, give me five minutes before you leave. I'll come up with a reason for you to return to London, and a means for you to let me know when assistance is on the way. Keep your head, keep your countenance. No heroics. Getting the information to Vaizey is what matters."

"Understood. Just let me know what's needed. Otherwise, er—what's that thing of that chap about service?"

"'They also serve who only stand and wait'?"

It was pleasing how easily da Silva picked up his meaning. "Yes. I always rather struggle with that."

"Do you? It sounds like my ideal job." Da Silva gave him a swift smile, without the usual hint of mockery, picked up his coat, and went silently down the stairs.

Curtis sank back against the wall and wondered what in the blue blazes was happening to him.

Da Silva, a secret agent. It seemed extraordinary when one considered the ghastly floral buttonholes and the languorous manner. Easier to imagine him as a competent professional if he thought of him working in the library, intent on his manuscript. Impossible to think about if he pictured him on his knees...

Enough of that. Sir Maurice, Curtis's uncle, would not have recruited da Silva if he wasn't good. For a moment Curtis imagined the two of them in a room: the ferocious Sir Maurice, who made Curtis's own spine stiffen; da Silva languid in a velvet jacket. His mind rebelled at the picture. But of course da Silva would adopt another persona for work, no doubt a crisp professional manner. He could pull it off, Curtis was sure, he switched between roles like an actor. Perhaps it was easier for queer sorts to play a variety of parts, being used to concealing the truth about themselves—

The thought pulled him up short.

He had been in exclusively male company at school, of course, and at college. He could have sought out female companionship at Oxford, as many did, but he had been occupied elsewhere, concentrating on his sporting career and, as a poor second, getting his degree. He had joined the army straight out of university, and from then on he'd mostly been in one or another part of Africa, at least up until Jacobsdal. He had, in fact, spent his life with men. And if, in those circumstances, one played the fool with other fellows, as he had at school, and college, or had a particular friend, as he had in the army, well, that was only natural. Men had needs.

Today's business with da Silva was very far from his first time with another chap. It was simply the first time he'd been forced to think about it.

Curtis shut his eyes. He could still feel a slight dampness in his groin from da Silva's mouth, and he had a momentary urge to stroke himself.

He had never considered his own tastes beyond the moment. He didn't often consider himself at all, not being the introspective sort. But in that shocking moment when he had thought he had forced himself on an unwilling man, he had faced a truth.

He had wanted da Silva. Not just the physical relief, not just a hand on his cock; he'd wanted the dark, clever man who dropped to his knees so easily for all his prickly pride. Curtis had woken up hard this morning, thinking of da Silva between his thighs in the mirror last night. He had struggled to control his arousal in the billiard room, watching the man bent over the green baize table. And nothing on earth could have held him back just now, not once da Silva had offered his outrageous, marvellous mouth.

You asked him to suck you off. You begged him to.

He rubbed his hands over his face, unsure where his thoughts were going.

Very well: he would rather have his cock sucked than not, and da Silva was a handsome devil who knew his way around a chap, and God knew it had been so long since he'd felt aroused, let alone acted on it. Was there anything more to it, really?

All his previous encounters had been with chaps like himself: soldiers, sportsmen, good fellows. He had an unformed but definite idea that being queer entailed doing something different, womanish, something like the rouged men in those London clubs. Like da Silva, with his perfectly shaped brows and tight trousers and mannerisms.

Curtis wasn't like that. He simply didn't *feel* queer, whatever that might feel like. He felt like a normal chap who, now and then, enjoyed encounters with other chaps, that was all. Some people might not see the distinction, he supposed, but there was definitely a difference. He wasn't sure what it was, but there was one. Well, there had to be, since he wasn't queer.

This was not a useful line of thought.

Curtis straightened up from the wall and marched downstairs to grab his oilskins. It was time to go back to the house, face the Armstrongs, do his duty to King and country, put away this self-indulgent nonsense. If da Silva could keep his mind on the job in hand, Archie Curtis, late of His Majesty's service, could hardly do less.

Chapter Eight

Luncheon was a noisy, chatty affair. Curtis concentrated on the interplay around him, viewing the country house party through the prism of what he knew.

Lambdon had his eye on Mrs. Grayling. No question of that; he was a heavy flirt, and rather a vulgar one. Curtis would have objected in Grayling's shoes, but the silly fellow was fascinated by Lady Armstrong. James Armstrong and Holt were still in friendly competition for Miss Carruth's attention. She divided her favours with a pleasant smile for both, but no sign that she felt any inclination towards either. A good dissembler, or simply not attracted to a pair of young men who were coming to strike Curtis as rather ill-mannered? Da Silva was charming the pallid Mrs. Lambdon, God alone knew why. Curtis did his best not to watch him. He couldn't help feeling his mouth looked a trifle bruised.

The rain stopped as they ate, and after coffee and cigars, Lady Armstrong assembled her walking party to the caves. Curtis, by now desperate for a bit of physical exertion, was among them; da Silva, he was unsurprised to note, was not. He was doubtless up to something. Curtis had found the dark lantern and his discarded pullover in his wardrobe before luncheon. He had no idea when da Silva had retrieved them or sneaked them in to his room, but it was a rather pleasing reminder of his competence. Curtis had forgotten all about them both.

Holt and Armstrong cut Miss Carruth out of the main group with a practised pincer movement, so Curtis walked most of the way with Miss Merton. It was no chore. She was, it turned out, not just a companion: she was the Patricia Merton who had taken gold at the Ladies' All England shooting competition for three years running, and the two-mile walk became as pleasant an interlude as almost any Curtis had spent since his return from South Africa.

As they paced through the open countryside, bare and bleak, with the hills ranging away up to the looming Pennine peaks, they spoke of target and game shooting, compared notes on gun models and cartridge manufacturers, argued the merits of pigeons and pheasants. Miss Merton animated proved to be a very likeable woman, not pretty, but handsome, with fine eyes and a decided, practical way about her, and she was remarkably easy to talk to. In fact, she was just the sort of woman he'd imagined he might marry, at some unspecified point in the future, although even by the end of that very enjoyable walk, he didn't feel any urge to bring that point closer.

Miss Merton showed no more inclination to cast lingering looks than Curtis felt. She discussed guns like a sensible woman, and kept half an eye on Miss Carruth, and after all, a new friendship was a much more appealing prospect than a mere country-house flirtation.

Lady Armstrong stopped them at the base of a rocky slope. "We go up here to the cave mouth. I hope everyone is ready for a little scramble, and nobody is afraid of the dark?" There was a ripple of laughter from everyone except Mrs. Lambdon, who gave a whinny of distress. Lady Armstrong smiled. "Perhaps the gentlemen could assist the ladies?"

Holt deftly swooped on Miss Carruth. Lady Armstrong gave her stepson a pitying smile and said, "James, support your mamma." Mr. Lambdon took Mrs. Grayling's arm with an intimate murmur that won him a giggle, leaving Mr. Grayling to offer his arm to Mrs. Lambdon. Curtis looked round at Miss Merton.

"Don't you dare," she told him.

"I shouldn't dream of it. You may need to help me if the going's too rough."

In fact the path was very manageable, and his leg not too bad at all. The cave entrance had been opened wide, and lamps hung there for the visitors' use. James and Lady Armstrong set off first. She nearly slipped on a smooth stone, and he caught her with a protective arm round her waist and a cry of "Watch out, mater!" At the same moment, Curtis almost lost his footing, as a drip from the ceiling splashed onto his head.

"All very treacherous, isn't it?" murmured Miss Merton. "Any idea what we're in for?"

"Well, it's a limestone cave, which is to say, the rainwater soaks through the ground and leaches out the stone. So we should see some rather good rock formations, I think."

They moved down through the first tunnel, which was steep and unpleasantly slippery, despite crude steps that had been cut underfoot. It was damp and cold and airless, and the walls seemed to bulge like ripples of flesh with a wet shine to their yellow-brown surface.

"Like being in the gullet of a dragon," Miss Carruth called back, voice echoing oddly off the wet walls. She was just behind the Armstrongs, followed by Grayling and Mrs. Lambdon, with Curtis and Miss Merton after them. "Oh!"

"What? Fen?" Miss Merton called. "Fen!"

Mrs. Lambdon ahead of them stopped dead, with a squeak of amazement.

"Do move, will you," said Miss Merton. "Oh. Oh, goodness me. Look at that."

It was one of the better caves Curtis had seen. Great spikes of stone came down from the roof like teeth, or sprouted up from the floor, looking like huge dribbled candles. The Armstrongs, familiar with the sight, had moved their lanterns to the best points to cast light. Shadows jumped and flickered. Mrs. Lambdon made a wailing noise and clutched Mr. Grayling's arm.

"Well, this is something." Miss Merton looked around. "Can we explore?"

"Please do," said Lady Armstrong. "There's a network of tunnels and galleries here like a honeycomb under the hills, but most of them are too narrow to go down very far. Don't squeeze through anything tight and you can't get lost. If your lantern should go out"—Mrs. Lambdon moaned—"just call out and stay still. It's very easy to get disoriented underground, or in the dark."

The party spread out. Curtis, intrigued and not burdened with a woman who wanted his support, headed down a wide tunnel into what turned out to be a small gallery, its walls an icy white compared to the brown and yellow of the main cave. He paced its edges, examining the rippled walls, imagining the age of the extraordinary creation. At the end of the gallery was a small wall of rocks, man made, and as he peered over he saw that it marked a pit, almost perfectly round, utterly black, nearly six feet wide.

He held out his lantern and peered down, but saw only the void gaping beneath. It was an unsettling sight. He dropped in a pebble experimentally and listened out, but heard no rattle as it hit bottom.

Footsteps sounded behind him.

"Good, isn't it?" Holt had come in alone. "Watch out for that pit. Nasty little trap. You wouldn't want to fall in."

Curtis straightened. "I wonder how far it goes down."

"Nobody knows. They've lowered ropes with lanterns on, but they've always run out of rope before they run out of hole. It's some kind of sinkhole. A bottomless pit, straight down to the bowels of the earth." Holt spoke with relish.

"Good Lord." Curtis stared into the abyss a moment longer. "Have you lost Miss Carruth to Armstrong?"

"To her bulldog." Holt pursed his lips, making a face intended to evoke Miss Merton's severity. Curtis had no patience with those manners; one did not speak of women like that. He gave the fellow a disapproving look and turned again to the weird walls.

Holt didn't seem to take the hint. "I say, quite seriously, what did you make of that business with our Hebrew friend this morning?"

"He beat you fair and square. What else is there to make of it?"

"Oh, come. That was professional play. Didn't you think? Have you ever seen a gentleman play like that?"

Curtis hadn't. If da Silva wasn't a professional sharp it wasn't for lack of ability, or an excess of morals either. It was quite obvious that he wasn't a gentleman. Holt was right.

Curtis couldn't bring himself to say it.

"He's a fine player," he said instead, defensively. "He didn't play for money. I don't see any reason to do the chap down. He may not be our sort but he's not so bad as all that."

"He's a blasted Jew."

"Well, yes, but what of it? That was a game of billiards, not a religious discussion."

Holt shook his head, annoyed at Curtis's lack of understanding. "You were a soldier. You must have some interest in protecting your country."

"Against da Silva?"

"Against his sort." Holt must have read Curtis's incomprehension in his face, because he went on, "This country is in the doldrums. Decadence is rotting us from within. We've a king who only cares for pleasure, and a set of adulterous commoners and wastrels and rootless cosmopolitan money-grubbers around him. Decent Britons scarcely get a look-in, nobody gives a curse for the people who make up the backbone of the Empire. The people who are supposed to set an example are all swept up in rackety living, or talking airy-fairy tripe about being sensitive, and the people with a bit of moral backbone are called old-fashioned. Well, I'd rather be old-fashioned if da Silva's an example of the modern type. I'd have hoped you were the same."

"I've no opinion on His Majesty's conduct and I'm not acquainted with his set," said Curtis stiffly. "As for the rest, I dare say you've a point." A fair point, he might have thought a few days ago, and perhaps nodded along, but it was ringing rather hollow now. "Nevertheless—"

"Nevertheless what? You don't approve of this sort of thing, do you?" Holt swept a hand, indicating the other members of the party, spread through the caves. "Blind pursuit of pleasure and self-indulgence, without a thought for their country. I should like to see them get what's coming to them."

"What is coming to them?" Curtis didn't quite like the look in Holt's eyes, which suggested the political fanatic, or possibly the religious kind.

"Oh, none of this will last. This country is heading for a crash, mark my words. There are other nations rising, ones with stronger, purer ideals and men who are prepared to work, to aspire. If we don't set ourselves to join them now, it won't be long before we face them on the battlefield. And we'll be better off doing either without parasites sapping our strength from within."

Curtis had heard this kind of talk a few times, and never from men who had actually put on a uniform. Normally a patient man, he had found armchair warriors almost intolerable since Jacobsdal, and there was a snap in his voice as he replied, "Yes, jolly good. So, when that conflict comes, will you be joining the army? Or, why not now, if you're so keen?"

Even in the lantern light he could see Holt's cheeks darken. "There's more than one way for a man to serve his country."

Curtis thought of da Silva's secret, thankless work doing exactly that, serving his country while others talked about it, and felt his mutilated hand curl to a half-fist. "That's right, there is. And there's more than one way for a man to serve his God too."

Holt's nostrils flared with anger. "Well. Armstrong said you were getting tight with the fellow. If you prefer to mix with Yids and dagos, I suppose that's your privilege."

Curtis turned on his heel and walked off. The light bobbed along the cave walls, illuminating the lumps and bulges of slick stone, strange shapes springing from shadows. The beauty of it passed him by. There was a man's low murmur and a feminine giggle from another passage, running off the mouth of the white gallery. He didn't look round.

The fact was, he *would* rather have had da Silva's company than Holt's. He should have liked to see wonder on his face, and to hear what a poet might make of this extraordinary place. He should have liked to explain how the limestone shapes were created, since he felt quite sure that would fall outside da Silva's area of expertise. He wanted to know how these weird sculptures of time would affect the imagination that had created things moving in the dark water of fishponds. He thought da Silva would enjoy it, and he thought his enjoyment would be real and interesting.

Miss Merton and Miss Carruth were perched on a rock in the main cave when he returned, marvelling at the ceiling. He headed for them rather than Mrs. Lambdon and Mr. Grayling, who stood together without conversation, examining the walls in a disconsolate fashion. Miss Merton gave her companion a frown as Curtis approached.

"No, Fen," she said firmly.

"Oh, Pat, don't be strict." Miss Carruth pouted. "Mr. Curtis, I'm desperate to know. The account of the caves in that wonderful book—is it true? Was it like this?"

One of his uncle's travelling companions had written a colourful account of the trip to the diamond mines that had made Sir Henry Curtis rich and famous twenty-five years ago. Curtis was used to being asked to verify some of the less plausible details. "It was true, yes. The natives used a cave very like this to entomb their dead kings around a table under drips of limestone. Turning them into human stalagmites."

Miss Carruth shuddered pleasurably. Miss Merton gave him a look. "Are you *quite* sure that's true? It seems very impractical and rather dramatic."

"Mr. Quatermain did have a flair for the dramatic," Curtis admitted. "Hence the success of the book. But my uncle is a very truthful man."

Lambdon returned from a side passage, escorting Mrs. Grayling, who looked a little flushed. Miss Merton made a clicking noise with her tongue, very quietly. James and Lady Armstrong followed from the direction of the white gallery, with Holt behind them, and the party set off back down the hill and over the moors towards Peakholme and tea.

Curtis was dressing for dinner when there was a rap on the door. If that was that bloody encroaching servant Wesley come to offer his services... He called, "Yes?" in a less than welcoming tone.

"Good evening," murmured da Silva, slipping in.

"Oh," Curtis said. "Hello."

"Nominally, and in the unlikely event of watchers through the mirror, I'd like to borrow a collar stud."

Curtis fished one out. "Here you are. Any progress?"

"I have plans for this evening." Da Silva pocketed the stud. "Rub your leg a bit tonight, as if the knee hurts, will you? I thought we might send you back tomorrow needing to see your specialist. Overexertion with that unwise trip to the caves."

"That's a jolly good idea, but—tomorrow?"

"The quicker you get to Vaizey, the better."

"Of course." Curtis swallowed. Naturally he wanted to leave this hellish house of intrigue and its good chaps and charming ladies. Naturally, he knew that crucial information had to be carried and he was the man to do it. It was just...

Da Silva was speaking. "If you ask him to wire me warning of the relief's arrival, he'll know what to say."

"Right. Will do."

"You look like a Viking who's been hit on the head without the benefit of a helmet. Are you all right?"

"Fine." Da Silva gave him a slight frown. Curtis managed a smile. "Fine. A little annoyed, that's all. I had a rather unpleasant talk with Holt earlier."

Da Silva's eyebrow flicked up. "Is he capable of any other kind?"

"Not to you, I should think. How do you tolerate that sort of thing?"

"I'm terribly rude, in situations where people can't hit me. What did he say to annoy you so?"

"Oh, nothing worth repeating. I'll get that excuse underway for tomorrow."

"Good." Da Silva hesitated by the door. He was sleeked and primped, dressed for elegant battle, with an outrageous frilly bloom in his buttonhole, but the undone collar, wings loose, revealed the hollow at the base of his neck, and Curtis couldn't take his eyes off it. He wanted to see da Silva undressed, dishevelled, undefended. He could almost feel the sensation of pulling open his white shirt, popping stud after stud, to reveal that pierced nipple, and pressing his face to the smooth skin. The need was on him out of nowhere, so strong that he could barely breathe.

"Do you need assistance?" da Silva asked, and for a fraction of a second Curtis couldn't tell what he was offering.

"The collar studs? No. I can manage." Curtis cursed himself as the words left his mouth. Of course he could manage, of course he didn't need those agile fingers working around his neck and down his chest, but...

"Are you sure?" Da Silva's eyes were on his, and his voice was just a little breathy. Curtis's mouth went dry.

"It, uh..." He couldn't think of anything to say but he held out a hand, his own studs in the palm, towards da Silva and saw his eyes flicker down and up again.

Da Silva plucked the studs off his palm and moved over, softly, standing very close, so close Curtis imagined he could feel the warmth of his slim body. He lifted his hands to Curtis's throat, nudging his chin up with a knuckle, and then, very slowly, ran the back of his finger down his neck, over his Adam's apple, delving just a fraction under the cloth of his shirt.

Da Silva reached up to fix the stud. He hooked a finger into the front of the collar and tugged gently, and Curtis swayed forward in helpless response.

"Mmm." Da Silva's breath was warm, tickling his skin. "I should probably apologise."

"What for?" Curtis managed.

"I distressed you." Da Silva's fingertip stroked the beginnings of stubble. "That business earlier was a trifle hectic. It wasn't my intention to cause you upset."

"You didn't." Curtis felt the skin of his throat moving against da Silva's finger as he spoke.

"I think I did, a little." Da Silva's lips curved in that secret smile. "I hope it was upset of the pleasanter sort."

Curtis gave a convulsive swallow. Da Silva made a face, looking a touch annoyed. "I beg your pardon. I didn't come in to bring that up." He slipped the stud deftly, impersonally into place, closing off Curtis's neck with the starched material. "Quite seriously, I'd hate you to worry on my account. Be assured, you need not."

"I shan't. Wait." Curtis reached out as da Silva made to move, putting a hand to his shoulder before he was even sure what he was going to do. Da Silva stopped at once, unnervingly motionless, eyes watchful. "May I assist you? In return?"

Da Silva hesitated. Curtis said, in the lightest tone he could, "Do allow me. Please." It wasn't nearly light enough.

Da Silva's lips parted, then curled. "I'd be most grateful."

He took the stud from his waistcoat pocket with two deft fingers and dropped it in Curtis's extended palm, then lifted his face, eyes on Curtis's, mouth so close. Curtis's breath caught. If he just leaned forward now—

He'd never kissed a man in his life, that bit of playacting in the library aside, and that had been none of his choice and over before it began. To do it himself, to lean forward and bring his mouth to another man's...that was unthinkable. Or, at least, he'd never acted on any such thought. Tossing a fellow off was one thing, a practical matter, but to kiss a man, as a lover— that felt like an irrevocable step, a terrifying one.

He wanted to do it. He wanted to kiss da Silva, wanted to see what he would taste like, how his lips would feel. He had no idea if da Silva kissed other men.

Da Silva was still watching him, waiting. Curtis swallowed, throat tight in the constraining material, then took the wings of the collar, allowing his fingers just to touch the warm skin. He could feel the pulse fluttering in da Silva's neck.

"You've very careful," da Silva murmured. "Interesting."

"Why interesting?" Curtis threaded the stud through the hole, conscious of the ugly shape of his leather-clad, mutilated hand.

"Well. That Viking build." Da Silva's eyes flickered down the length of his body and up again. "That delightful, masterful, soldierly way of yours. I expected a more, shall we say, bull-at-a-gate approach. Conquering by brute force. And instead you're sliding it in, bit by bit, so very carefully and gently that I can hardly feel the penetration—"

Curtis fumbled the stud. The back half sprang from his fingers and dropped to the floor. He stared at da Silva, open-mouthed, and saw him glance up from under long dark lashes with unmistakable mischief.

"You utter sod," Curtis said.

"Sorry." Da Silva held a hand up to stop him from speaking. "I *am* sorry, that wasn't fair. You—well, you're quite the temptation, you know."

"I want to see you again," Curtis blurted out.

"See?" Da Silva's well-shaped brow arched. Curtis was sure he plucked them, and didn't care. They were beautiful. Da Silva was beautiful, and standing painfully close, and Curtis could have reached out and pulled him into his arms—

"You know what I mean." He took a deep breath. "I've a favour to return."

Da Silva's eyes widened, lips parting, and now Curtis was quite sure that he could press his own lips to that tantalising mouth, that da Silva would meet him there, if he could only make himself take the step. He swallowed. "Do you—do you think they're watching now?"

"Christ, I hope not."

"Then—"

"No." Da Silva's smile was rather crooked. "That is—a delightful offer, my dear, and I can't tell you how much I should like to accept, but, and I hesitate to point this out, *not queer*, hmm?"

Curtis couldn't give a damn at this moment. He had other concerns. "Why don't you let me worry about that?"

"Oh God, I'd love to." Da Silva's eyes were so dark, ridiculously dark. Eyes a fellow could drown in, and Curtis might not be practised in these matters but he couldn't mistake the desire he saw in them.

"Then—" He made a fractional movement forward, and da Silva stepped back and away.

"I'd love to, *but*, believe it or not, I do have some decent impulses." His mouth twisted. "You need to go to London tomorrow, and deal with your uncle, and do the things that gentlemen do. I have work to do here tonight. And the dinner gong has been struck. Duty calls." He turned and whisked out of the room before Curtis could speak, leaving him staring.

He took a deep breath, bent, with some difficulty, to pick up the abandoned stud, then sat on the bed and put his head in his hands.

He was going back down to London tomorrow. He would tell Sir Maurice everything, or at least, most of it. He would ensure help was sent—able-bodied help, people who would handle things like professionals. That would be the end of his involvement.

He would never see da Silva again.

He could find him, of course. He could go among the Bohemian types, poets and painters and sculptors and arty sorts. He could seek him in the clubs where men danced with men. He could go into the East End, into the narrow, poorly lit lanes where dark faces filled crowded shops, looking for the locksmith's son.

And what would he do once he'd found him?

They had nothing whatsoever in common, of race or society or taste or intellect. Velvet jackets and poetry readings were as far from his experience as shooting parties and military talk were from da Silva's, and Curtis had never had any time for the Bohemian set.

No, this was not an acquaintance it would be possible or sensible to carry on.

And yet... He liked the man, that was the truth of it. It wasn't just this—whatever it was, between them that he wanted to pursue. He liked his sense of humour and his quick intelligence and his dedication. Liked his mouth, and those clever fingers, and the desire, for *him*, that had smouldered in those dark eyes...

Stop this. You've work to do, he told himself. *Concentrate on the job. Da Silva's not sitting next door thinking about you.*

That was the wrong mental image to have conjured up. For a brief moment Curtis pictured da Silva, naked and tousled, lying back on the bed with dark eyes hooded and one hand stroking himself, then cut off the thought savagely.

It took him several minutes to get his cufflinks in. His hand kept shaking.

Chapter Nine

Dinner was a noisy affair. Lady Armstrong and Mrs. Grayling both bubbled with high spirits, and James Armstrong was in a crowing, boisterous sort of mood. Fenella Carruth exclaimed at length on the wonders of the cave and assured da Silva he should have come. His appalled response seemed genuine.

"Good heavens, no. Not at gunpoint. I don't take Underground trains, far less descend into the depths of the uncivilised earth."

"Really?"

"Dear child, I can't bear *cellars.*"

"Scared of the dark, are you?" said James.

Da Silva lifted his eyes in a soulful gaze. "Man was born to walk on the surface of the earth, not its underside. Our nature is to aspire to the sun, and gaze at the stars."

Mrs. Lambdon clucked in support of that sentiment. Holt and James Armstrong looked, not unreasonably, nauseated. Curtis wondered how da Silva got away with it, since anyone who'd read his poetry would know he didn't go in for anything like that sort of claptrap, but of course no one present would have done anything of the sort. One more of da Silva's private jokes.

Miss Carruth begged Curtis to retell his uncle's story of the Kukuana Place of Death from that blasted book, and as other voices joined in, he felt it would support his character as a good fellow to oblige. He described first the chamber of which he had heard so much, with the great stone table, and at its head a statue of a colossal skeleton, fifteen feet in height. It rose from its seat, spear held above its head, ready to strike. And round the menacing thing's table, guests at Death's feast, sat the kings of the Kukuanas.

"All twenty-seven of them," he said. "Each seated under a drip of water, running down onto their heads, turning them to stone drop by drop. Shrouded in white spar. One could see their features still through the veil of stone. Twala, the king that my uncle killed, sat in his chair with his head in his lap—"

There was a general shriek from the women, followed by cries of pleasurable protest. "So horrible," said Miss Carruth with a wriggle.

"So exotic and—and heroic," exclaimed Mrs. Grayling.

"So disgusting," said da Silva, and Curtis saw with surprise that he looked rather sick. "To spend one's eternal rest seated underground—"

"We all end up underground," Lambdon pointed out bluffly.

"But to *sit* under the earth, round the devil's dining table, with water dripping on one's head. What a revolting practice." He shuddered. Curtis made a mental note to tell him about the Tibetan tradition of sky burial, which was even less appropriate for the dinner table than the Kukuana rituals, and realised that of course he'd never have the chance.

He attempted to be companionable that evening, proposing a game of whist to the younger men. Grayling was enthusiastic; Holt and Armstrong exchanged a flicker of a glance and made excuses.

That gave Curtis pause. James Armstrong was going to gaol. His antipathy didn't matter a jot. But Holt was not involved in the Armstrongs' crimes. He was a sportsman, a good mixer, he seemed to have entry to wide social circles. Suppose he had complained to his friend of the earlier disagreement, and Armstrong, the bumptious oaf, had dropped a hint? *I say,*

*Curtis and that dago are rather tight, aren't they? — Tight? You
don't know the half of it.*

If Armstrong talked, and Holt chose to play the rumour-
monger, Curtis could be in for unpleasantness.

He felt sweat prickle along his hairline. He had no idea how
da Silva could live with such poise, threatened by exposure at
every corner. He felt he would go grey within a week.

The night's sleep, unbroken by burglary, was welcome, but
Curtis rather regretted his healthy look in the mirror the next
morning, since he had to make a fuss about his knee. He
limped into the breakfast room, from which da Silva was absent
yet again, and fielded an array of sympathetic queries.

"It's my own fault," he insisted to Lady Armstrong's
apologies. "I overdid it. But I'm a little worried, to be honest. I
may have thrown the kneecap out on the rough ground."

"Shall I call the doctor?"

"I think I should see my specialist in London, I'm afraid."
Curtis adjusted his features to a look of regret. "It's something
of a tricky case."

Lady Armstrong gave cries of distress and vexation and
sent a heavy-eyed James Armstrong for a Bradshaw's railway
guide, which was when Curtis realised it was a Sunday.

"There's only one passenger train to London the whole day.
You could make it, just, but it's a cursed bad one," Sir Hubert
said, frowning. "Stops everywhere."

"And that will do your knee no good," Lady Armstrong put
in solicitously. "I fear you must wait until Monday, Mr. Curtis.
Do telephone for an appointment, won't you?"

Curtis allowed himself to be persuaded. He had no desire to
spend nine hours on a stopping train to London. And, a voice at

the back of his mind pointed out, he might have a chance for a talk with da Silva.

With that as a prospect, and his character as an invalid to support, Curtis declined to attend church. Everyone else was packed off in a procession of motorcars, except for Holt and Armstrong, who announced they would go for a tramp. They both looked tired, but pleased with themselves. Likely they'd made a private night of it and were off to find a pub.

With the house to himself, Curtis set off to the library.

Da Silva wasn't there. He wasn't in the breakfast room, and he didn't appear to be in any of the drawing rooms. He surely couldn't be sleeping in past ten, Curtis thought with disapproval and, feeling just a little sensation of heart in mouth, went to knock on his bedroom door.

There was no answer.

Curtis hesitated. But he did need to speak to the fellow. He turned the handle experimentally, and the door opened.

Da Silva's room was empty.

Curtis looked around, bewildered. No unguents or studs on the dresser, no sign of occupancy. He opened the wardrobe, then the drawers. They were all empty.

It seemed that da Silva had left.

What the devil?

Curtis retreated to his own room to think. Da Silva had been up to something last night. Had he decided to change the plan? To abstract sufficient evidence of blackmail and treachery to hang the Armstrongs, along with the incriminating photographs, and disappear in the night, without a word?

Curtis wouldn't put that past him. What he would put past him was the ability to leave the house in the night, and cover thirty miles to Newcastle—

Where there were no trains today except the milk train and that stopping train. Curtis felt quite sure da Silva would have checked Bradshaw before disappearing, and would have taken a decent train rather than one that went less than the speed of an Austin motorcar. In any case, how would he have got to the station, with his portmanteau? He couldn't drive, Curtis doubted he could cover thirty miles overnight, and he could not imagine da Silva hiding out on the moors to avoid pursuit.

He went back into da Silva's deserted room. This time he locked the door behind him and proceeded to search thoroughly, getting down to the floor and checking under the furniture. He wasn't sure what he was looking for, except that he had an increasing feeling something was wrong.

He found it behind the dresser. Da Silva's flashlight.

It was cylindrical, of course. It could have rolled off a surface and been forgotten, except the bulb still worked. Except that da Silva was too careful a man to leave such things lying around. Except...

He did not like this, not at all.

He told himself he was being nonsensical, and made himself go down to the library again, where he read through *The Fish-pond* as if it might provide some sort of clue. He wished he could go up to the folly—not that he rationally thought da Silva would be waiting there; still, the urge nagged at him—but he had to keep up the pretence of his bad knee.

He made himself wait until lunchtime, with da Silva still absent, before enquiring as airily as he could, "Where's the poet? Communing with his muse?"

"Mr. da Silva? He, ah, left early this morning." Lady Armstrong threw him a meaningful look.

James Armstrong gave an ostentatious cough that sounded like, "Asked." Rapid glances of delighted shock flashed round the table.

"James." Sir Hubert's tone was warning.

"Well, honestly," James began, and subsided at his father's frown, adding a mumbled, "I did say, though, mater."

"Enough of that." Sir Hubert set about talking golf. Curtis pretended to listen, thinking frantically.

The implication was clear: da Silva had been evicted for some crime against hospitality. Stealing the silver, buggering the footman, breaking into his host's private files. It was, of course, possible that he'd been caught prowling and packed off, and that would explain how his possessions had been removed. And yet, and yet...

It was an hour's drive to Newcastle station. The milk train left at half past three in the morning; surely da Silva would not have been thrown out at such an hour. But if he had been sent to cool his heels on the station platform waiting for the morning's stopping train, might the Armstrongs not have mentioned it when Curtis proposed to catch the same train? And wouldn't Curtis have heard a car returning at some point this morning?

There was nothing conclusive here, nothing he could pin down, but the hairs on the back of his neck were rising.

He set himself to be as convivial as he could for the rest of the meal, and observed to Lady Armstrong that he rather thought his leg might be feeling better. "I dare say you'll think I'm a dreadful worrier for making such a fuss—"

"Oh heavens, no! I do know how it is when one has a nagging complaint," Lady Armstrong assured him. Mrs. Lambdon, animated by that, launched into an account of her own chronic health problems, which saved Curtis the effort of doing anything but nodding courteously along.

The rest of the day seemed to last forever. Curtis took a stroll round the grounds. He gave the excuse that he wanted to see if his knee was damaged or simply strained by the previous day's walk.

There was, so far as he could see, no disturbed ground under the redwoods, no evidence of a shallow grave or a deep one, and he cursed da Silva and his vivid turns of phrase even as he let himself into the folly. That was empty too. It smelled of cold stone and wood must. It ought to have smelled of male sweat, and spunk, and the stuff da Silva used on his hair.

The absurd thought came to Curtis that if something had happened to da Silva, if there had been foul play, he would never touch his hair again. His throat tightened crazily then, and he stood alone in the desolate folly, choked by the absence of a man he barely knew.

The endless, horrible day dragged on. Curtis ranged over the grounds till twilight fell, seeing nothing, then retreated to the library again before dinner, because the presence of the other guests was beginning to scrape on his nerves like barbed wire on skin. He was staring at a page of an Oppenheim novel he thought he'd read before when Armstrong and Holt came in.

"We're looking for Grayling," Armstrong said. He seemed a little more friendly than he had the previous night. "Want to make a fourth at billiards?"

"I'll pass, thanks."

"Missing your partner?" asked Holt with a touch of nastiness.

"Who, da Silva? Hardly. I like to win now and again." He was not in the mood for this bloody pointless banter, the endless meaningless chaff of people without purpose or employment in life. Holt was right about that much; it was no way for men to live. Although Holt seemed to enjoy it well enough.

Another day, and he would leave this damned place, Curtis told himself. One more day to look for da Silva.

Recklessly, he asked Armstrong, "What happened there? Pinching the spoons, was he?"

Holt glanced at Armstrong and opened his mouth, but Armstrong was already replying cheerfully, "Caught him fuzzing the cards. Holt was quite right about him being a sharp, you know."

"Well, by God," Curtis said. "I owe you an apology, Holt, you're quicker on the uptake than I. I was quite in the dark about that."

Armstrong gave a bray of laughter. "You're not the only one in the dark. Eh, Holt?"

"Don't talk nonsense," Holt snapped. "What about that game, Curtis?"

Curtis indicated his knee in answer, and the younger men retreated. He thought he heard a very quiet murmur of subdued speech from the other side of the door as they left.

The earlier whisper of fear was now a scream. He did not believe that da Silva had been playing cards with Holt and Armstrong last night. If he had, it was just possible that he had been caught cheating—it was not the act that Curtis doubted, but the being caught in it. But in that case the two young men would have made a terrific fuss, which Curtis would have heard. It was out of the question that Holt would have let such a thing be brushed under the carpet. They were both lying.

That meant Holt was in on the business.

Curtis didn't know why he hadn't considered that before. James Armstrong was a boisterous fool, idling away his days in play. Holt had a brain, and a nasty streak. An up-and-coming man, a bright fellow, seeing James Armstrong's opportunities and helping him exploit them. Serving the decadents he despised with their just deserts.

Yes, Holt was in on it, Curtis was sure. He knew what was going on, and he hadn't liked that remark of Armstrong's just now. His smile had been false as hell, and he had changed the subject with a wrench. He should have been crowing at the story of da Silva caught cheating at cards. Instead, he'd led the talk away from Armstrong's words…

You're not the only one in the dark.

Curtis thought about that. He thought about the conversation last night, and da Silva's shuddering admission of his dislike of caves and underground spaces. Then he shut his eyes and breathed very deeply, because what he was thinking made him feel nauseated, and enraged, and terrified as he thought of that dreadful black sinkhole where a body might fall for miles…

And a little hopeful. Because there were those who wanted their enemies dead, and there were those who made them suffer first. Surely, if one hated a man, and knew that he feared dark caves, might one not leave him alive there, underground, at least for a while?

Curtis was never afterwards sure how he got through the rest of the evening. He made what must have been appropriate remarks. He ate, and drank. He did not spring on Holt or Armstrong and choke the lives out of the bastards. He went to bed early, and made himself sleep for two hours, and at one o'clock in the morning, he took the flashlight and moved as quietly as possible downstairs.

He let himself out of the kitchen door and set off for the caves, skirting round the gravel drive and stony paths for a good quarter-mile to avoid the carrying sound of crunching feet.

There was a sharp chill in the air and a half-moon in the sky. It was enough to see by. Others might have found the dark walk and the stretching moon shadows frightening. Curtis was fearful enough of what he might find in the caves not to give a damn. In any case, with the colour bleached from the landscape, the bare hills bore some resemblance to the scrublands of South Africa, and the knowledge that there was no Boer sniper behind a bush was enough by itself to make the walk seem relatively pleasant.

The landscape looked different at night of course, but he had a soldier's sense of direction, and he only missed his path once, losing just a few minutes. He covered the ground in not much over forty-five minutes, all told, and after a scramble up the hill, stood in the black cave mouth.

"Da Silva?" he called.

No response.

He took one of the lamps kept there and lit it, then set off into the cave. The light flickered madly with the swing of the lamp, creating grotesque shadows that leapt and jumped at him.

"Da Silva?" he called into the main cave. His voice echoed back.

He would have to search each gallery, he knew. He should do it logically, work his way round, but his mind kept coming back to that terrible black sinkhole and he took a few strides on the cold, slippery stone underfoot, towards the tunnel that led to the white gallery, and called again, "Da Silva!"

His voice rang off the wall and died away, and he heard a soft, quiet sound like a sob.

"Da Silva!" He raised the lantern high, hurrying as quickly as he dared over the treacherously smooth cave floor, and came into the white gallery and saw, sprawled on the floor, by the sinkhole, back against a stalagmite, the dishevelled form of a dark-haired man.

Then Curtis was over by him, on his knees on the freezing stone. Da Silva was soaking wet, hair sodden. His arms were stretched back behind him, around the horrible wet smoothness of the stone, and as Curtis registered the ropes around his wrists, he saw a droplet of water spatter from the ceiling onto da Silva's head, and saw his body jerk.

"Oh Christ." Curtis gathered him into his arms as best he could, given how tightly he was tethered to the rock. His skin was ice cold. "Da Silva, can you hear me? It's Curtis. I'm here. I'll get you out. Daniel?"

Da Silva's head was flopped forward against Curtis's chest. He made an incoherent noise. Curtis took his chin and tenderly tilted his head up. Water ran down his grey face. His eyes were shut.

"Daniel," said Curtis hopelessly.

Daniel's eyelids fluttered, then opened. The dark eyes locked on to Curtis's. He said, choking, "Don't be a dream. Don't. Please. Don't be—"

"I'm here. I've got you. I'm not a dream."

Daniel blinked. Water dripped from his dark lashes. He looked at Curtis for a long moment, and whispered, "You came. Oh God, you came."

"You made me come," said Curtis, and wrapped his arms tighter as Daniel broke into weak, helpless sobs.

He wasn't sure how long he held him, sprawled together on the cold wet stone, holding him away from the awful, relentless, hammering drips, but he was damned uncomfortable by the time Daniel's tears had turned to deep, ragged breathing.

"Who did this?" he asked.

"J-James and H-Holt." Daniel's teeth were chattering, but that was an improvement, Curtis knew. "Going to leave, leave, l-leave me here. Turn me to s-stone."

"Rubbish." Curtis clutched the dark, sopping hair. "That takes centuries. I need to let go, understand? I have to get you loose."

Daniel gave a tiny gasp, then shut his eyes and nodded. Curtis released him, reluctantly, and rose, stiff and wet. He took off his overcoat, draped it over Daniel's shaking body, still in evening dress, and went to get him free.

The rope that bound him was knotted round the other side of the stone. It wasn't tied in a particularly difficult way, but it was thick, and swollen with the endless water that ran down the side of the stalagmite. Curtis moved the lantern, heard Daniel's whimper, put it back so that the light shone on him, and hurried back to get another lamp from the cave entrance. With that illuminating the other side of the rock, he began to work at the knot.

"Curtis?" rasped Daniel. "Curtis?"

He leapt up and went round the rock. "What?"

"Just... Not a dream."

"No." Curtis put a hand to the cold cheek and felt Daniel's head turn, his lips brushing Curtis's skin. "I have to get this rope off you now. I'm here, and I won't leave you, but you have to let me work."

The worst part of fever dreams was always the help, he thought savagely: one's uncle, or the nurse, or one's friend, coming to bend over the bed with soothing words and a cool drink, and one felt comforted and cared for at last, and then one woke again to solitude and parching thirst and a night that seemed endless. Curtis didn't like to imagine what it must have been like to spend a full day here, in the dark, with that awful torture of the drips and the encroaching cold and wet, and to dream that help was here and wake again and again to hopelessness.

The knot was irretrievably stuck. He took out his pocketknife and sawed at the rope with vicious force.

"Curtis." It was a croak.

"Let me do this," he said through his teeth.

"*Curtis!*"

"Curtis," said a taunting voice from the other end of the cave.

He knelt there, totally still, for a second. Then he folded the pocketknife, put it down by the stalagmite and stood to face Holt.

Chapter Ten

Holt was hanging his lantern on a jutting bit of rock. The light of three lamps made the white gallery disturbingly bright. Curtis glanced down at Daniel, still pinioned, his eyes black pits in his drawn, fearful face, and looked up at the man who had done this to him.

"I hope you're proud of yourself," he said.

Holt gave him an incredulous look. "At least I'm not a bloody queer."

"You're a blackmailer. A torturer."

"Murderer," Daniel rasped.

"Who did you murder?" Curtis rolled his shoulders, making sure his Norfolk jacket was loose enough, and took a sideways step. Holt registered the movement and something leapt in his face. Eagerness, Curtis thought. He wanted a fight.

He'd get one.

Holt shed his overcoat, eyes on Curtis. "A couple of traitors. You should be happy about that, actually."

"Lafayette's men." Curtis began a circling motion, saw Holt mimic him, watched his gait. "The men who tampered with the guns that went to Jacobsdal. You blackmailed them to do it, did you?"

"No!" Holt sounded outraged by the accusation. "That was Armstrong. Nothing to do with me. A disgraceful business."

"But you murdered the men who did it? Why?"

"They were *traitors*." Holt sounded as though he was appealing for understanding. "And depraved with it. Filthy beasts. They liked girls, young ones. Disgusting. They deserved to die."

"There we agree. What did you do with them?" Curtis asked, as if he cared. "The sinkhole?"

"Down to the bowels of the earth. Makes it a useful place for disposal. Nobody's ever found the bottom, did I say?" Holt's eyes glittered in the lamplight and the reflections of white stone. "I thought I'd throw the Jew down alive tonight. He screams like a girl. I want to see how long I can hear him falling."

Daniel made an animal noise of sheer terror. Curtis rocked on the balls of his feet, flexing his fingers. Holt shook his head. "Are you really planning to fight over him? Good God. I would never have thought it of you, Curtis. A soldier, a man of breeding, a Blue, up to those filthy tricks. Aren't you ashamed of yourself?"

Curtis managed, "No." He took a couple of steps closer to Holt, who raised his fists, then gave a little laugh.

"It's a shame. I'd have liked to spar properly with you. I don't suppose it counts, thrashing a cripple."

"Don't worry about me." That was what Curtis meant to say, anyway, but his mouth wasn't quite working now, and the words came out oddly. He looked at his hands in the lamplight and saw that they were shaking.

Holt's smile vanished. "I hope you're not yellow." He sounded aggrieved. "You're not afraid of a scrap, are you? Lost your nerve in the war? Damn it, I've been looking forward to a real turn-up with you, and you're just another cowardly bugger. Where's the challenge in that? At least one can take some pleasure in kicking a Jew."

That was when Curtis went for him.

His uncle's writer friend, Quatermain, had made a great fuss about Sir Henry Curtis's Viking blood, and the Berserker spirit that came upon him in battle. Curtis felt that to be a ridiculous and romantic way of looking at matters. If he had been asked to describe his battle rage, he would not have called it "Berserker spirit". The phrase, he felt, was "homicidal mania".

There was no red mist, there was no period where he didn't know what he was doing, there was not even anger as he knew it normally. Instead, there was a strange detachment and an exquisite, savage pleasure in violence. He strode forward, seeing Holt's fists go up in approved style, as if he thought they were going to fight like gentlemen, and landed a low punch that just failed to connect with the man's balls, thanks to an impressively fast reaction from Holt. He leapt back, opened his mouth, and saw something in Curtis's face that warned him to waste no more breath on speech.

Then they were fighting in earnest, a savage, scrambling match, no Queensberry rules here, both slipping on the smooth wet rock underfoot, both knowing that a fall could mean defeat. They were evenly matched in size and weight, and Holt had earned his boxing blue, and kept in shape. He had the huge advantage of two full hands and used it well, with relentless attacks on Curtis's right side, forcing him to use the mutilated, less powerful fist that jarred painfully with each blow.

But Curtis had spent eight years in the army, fighting people who fought back, and he knew what would happen to Daniel if he lost, and, most of all, he was in a cold killing rage. He struck and struck again, disregarding the blows landed on him and the pain of his own fist, and watched blood spray from Holt's hate-filled mouth as an uppercut sent his head back.

Holt slipped and landed on his tailbone. Curtis took a step forward, drawing back his leg to kick his opponent's head like a rugby ball, and almost turned his ankle on an unseen dip in the ground. He staggered but retained his balance.

Holt scrabbled desperately backwards, to his coat on the rock, delved into it and produced a knife.

Curtis threw back his head and laughed, the sound booming off the cave walls. It was so perfectly, utterly comical.

He hoped Daniel was watching, he'd find it hilarious. Holt regained his feet, waving the blade, and Curtis wanted to ask, did he not see the irony, after all his fine words about English superiority, pulling what he would have been the first to call a dago trick.

Holt lunged at him with the knife. Curtis threw up his right arm, and the blade slid through cloth and burned on his skin, but that meant it was nowhere near Curtis's left as he snapped a blow into Holt's jaw, just where he'd placed the uppercut. He saw the jarring punch cloud Holt's eyes, and as it did, Curtis grabbed Holt's knife hand with his own left. He twisted himself round the other man, wrapping his brawny right arm around Holt's neck, and tightened his grip.

Holt choked and struggled. Curtis leaned back, taking his weight, digging his fingers into Holt's wrist till the knife fell. He took Holt's jaw with his freed hand, and twisted head against neck, until he felt the abrupt give and heard the crack.

He let go, and turned from the body before it hit the floor.

Daniel was sprawled by the rock, staring at him, eyes impossibly wide and dark. He looked terrified.

"Holt's dead now," Curtis tried to explain, in case that wasn't clear. The words still wouldn't come out properly, so he retrieved Holt's knife, a razor-edged thing better than his own pocketknife, and sliced through the binding rope with a couple of cuts.

Daniel tried to struggle away from the rock. Curtis knelt, helping him disentangle the ropes. They were both shaking.

Daniel was cold. That was it.

Curtis went back to Holt's corpse and stripped it to its drawers, fingers fumbling. He piled the mostly dry clothes on top of the body, for lack of anywhere else, and went to get Daniel's clothes off.

He wasn't much help. His hands would hurt, Curtis thought, noting the raw red marks round his wrists and the

130

grey, puffy look to his fingers, so he carefully peeled off the sodden evening jacket and waistcoat, then ripped open Daniel's wet shirt rather than bothering with the studs—that reminded him of something, but he wasn't sure what. Piece by piece, he stripped the soaking, shuddering man naked, and used Holt's undershirt to towel him as dry as he could, and then, with his hands on Daniel's cold, damp skin, that was when Curtis came back to himself.

He took a deep, sucking breath. "Jesus." His voice was hoarse.

"Curtis?" It was a whisper. Daniel's eyes were huge and fearful.

"God." He blinked away the remnants of the rage. "Hell. I, uh…"

Daniel tried to say something, and swayed and almost fell, and Curtis seized him and held him close, disregarding his nakedness, till the other man regained his balance and he could let go. He grabbed for Holt's clothes, fumbling each garment onto Daniel with fingers that felt like sausages but still worked better than the other man's. The sight of Daniel's hands without their quick deftness threatened to tip him back to fury.

Holt's clothes were too big, of course, but that was better than the alternative. He belted the trousers tightly round the slim waist, buttoned the Norfolk jacket and heavy overcoat. Holt's shoes were far too large; Daniel's own wet dress shoes would have to do, but he pocketed Holt's socks till they could find a place to dry his feet.

He picked up Daniel's discarded clothes, and threw them down the sinkhole, followed by the rope and Holt's shoes. He kept the knife. Last of all, he dragged the corpse over to the sinkhole.

Daniel made a noise in his throat. Curtis said, "Shut your eyes," because he was quite sure Daniel didn't need to see a body disappear into that dreadful well, and dropped Holt down into the dark.

Then he took Daniel out of the cave.

They had to pause at the entrance, for Curtis to replace the lanterns, and to find a dry rock where Daniel could sit, slumped forward, while Curtis carefully dried his feet with his handkerchief and fitted Holt's thick socks on.

Holt had arrived on a bicycle. It was a decent touring bike, but with no grip in his right hand and Daniel at best semiconscious, it was useless to him. Curtis considered the matter, then told Daniel, "Wait for me. I'll be back," and hauled the thing into the caves. The idea of throwing it down the sinkhole, on top of the body, seemed wrong, but he had no other choice, so he dropped it in.

For all he knew, Holt was still falling into the void.

Daniel was curled over when he came out again, arms wrapped round himself. Curtis looked at his sodden shoes and at his face, and said, "Hold on now," then he tied the shoes round his neck by the laces, and picked Daniel up in his arms.

It was not an easy walk. Daniel wasn't bulky, but he was not far off six feet tall, and he slipped out of consciousness within a few moments, so that he was dead weight. Curtis was uncomfortably aware that he couldn't afford to fall on the scree, in case his knee gave way. He was damned impressed with how it was holding up so far, in fact. Maybe the doctors had been right to tell him to use it more, although this might not have been quite the exercise they had intended.

He paced along the dimly moonlit road, step by step, with Daniel limp and heavy in his arms. His right fist hurt like hell, and he could feel blood trickling down his forearm where Holt had caught him with the knife, and he had no idea what to do now.

It was close to three in the morning. He would not make any decent speed with Daniel to carry. The Armstrongs would be expecting Holt back. Would James come looking?

Where should he go?

The only telephone for miles would be Peakholme's. Newcastle was thirty miles away. And he needed to get Daniel warm. He could ask for help if he saw a shepherd's hut or farmhouse, except that he had seen nothing at all for miles in this godforsaken bleak landscape, and he knew all too well the dangers of seeking shelter in enemy territory.

That thought led his tired mind to memories of scrambling through the brush in Boer territory, looking for somewhere to hole up, and then to the little rocky *kraal*, the ruins of a farmhouse topping a small isolated hill, where his handful of men had retreated...

Stone-walled, defensible ruins on a hill.

Was that a brilliant idea, or a terrible one? He wasn't sure. He wished Daniel was awake to ask. He wished Daniel was awake to walk. But since he wasn't, Curtis set his teeth and trudged on, one foot then another, covering the two miles back to Peakholme.

It was half past four when he got there, every part of him aching. From the last vantage point, he had seen no lights in the house. He had to skirt round through the woods to reach the folly without coming in sight of the windows, but he was reasonably sure he would not be troubled with gardeners at this hour. The last incline, up to the folly, with Daniel's weight working against him, was one of the hardest things he had ever done, each staggering step a defiance of gravity and exhaustion, but at last he was at the door, fumbling it open, getting Daniel inside.

He half-dragged him up the winding stairs, and there, spent, he flopped down on the oak floor, moved the other man to lie against him, and allowed his muscles to shriek their complaints.

After a few minutes, when the blood was no longer pounding quite so loudly in his ears, he checked Daniel. He was much warmer. The close contact had been good for that, at least, and Holt's blasted heavy overcoat was a good one. He checked Daniel's wrists and saw to his relief that the fingers looked normal again.

"Daniel?" he murmured.

Daniel's breathing was deep and even. He lay heavily in Curtis's arms, and Curtis hesitated, wondering if he might be permitted this, then slid his fingers over Daniel's face, barely touching, running them along the lines of his jaw and brow, over the skin of his cheeks, and finally, daringly, over his lips.

Curtis didn't expect him to wake, but Daniel's eyelids flickered and he gave a little moan. Curtis cursed his own selfishness. "It's all right," he murmured. "You're safe. Go back to sleep."

Daniel's mouth moved, then his eyes snapped open and he jerked convulsively. Curtis grabbed him to stop him struggling, realised that was a bad idea as he started to cry out, and slapped a hand over his mouth, feeling an utter swine as he stiffened with fear.

"It's Curtis, you're safe. Stop, damn it! You're safe, I've got you. Stop," he hissed, and felt Daniel slump back into his arms at last. He moved his hand away.

"Curtis?"

"Here."

"Curtis," Daniel repeated, with a hint of satisfaction. He shut his eyes again, and Curtis thought he was going to sleep, but after a few moments he said, "I was in the cave."

"Don't think about that."

"In the cave, in the dark. It—dripped. Over and over. And that hole—" His voice was shaking.

"Stop it. It's done."

"You came."

"Of course I did."

Daniel was silent a little longer, then he said, "Did you kill Holt?"

"Yes."

"Don't like violence. Doesn't solve anything."

Curtis shrugged. He felt that violence had solved that particular problem nicely. Daniel snuggled against him, muttering something that Curtis didn't catch, and within a few seconds he was asleep again.

Curtis half-lay with his head against cold stone and his body on a hard wood floor, feeling Daniel's heavy weight over him, warm and safe. He luxuriated in the sensation for a few moments before turning his mind to what came next.

He had to get Daniel out. Holt would be missed today. He would, he thought grimly, fight to the death before he let James Armstrong get his hands on Daniel again, but it might well come to that if he faced men with guns.

With two hands he would have stolen one of the Armstrongs' motors. Perhaps he still could, but it would be a noisy business, to break in and start the machine, and he would have to take the time to get Daniel into the seat. And he was not at all sure he could control a car at speed along these winding roads, gripping the wheel with only finger and thumb. Certainly not fast enough to outdistance a pursuer, and he felt sure that he would be chased.

It was an option, but one for desperation. What were the alternatives? He could try and place a telephone call—he could beg a lift to Newcastle and call from there, if his hosts were still keeping up the pretence of hospitality—but that meant leaving Daniel alone in the folly.

He stirred. Curtis stroked a soothing hand over his brow, and found it unpleasantly warm.

Christ, what if he was going to be ill? It would hardly be surprising if a day soaked in water led to a bad chill.

He needed food and water and blankets, then, and he would have to get them soon, before the house was up. He needed a gun. He would place a call to his uncle from here, whatever the risk, and summon help, and after that... Well, if need be he would retreat to the folly and hold it as a defensible position for as long as it took.

Curtis contemplated that prospect as he gently rolled Daniel off him. He took a quick look around and, to his delight, found that an old wooden chest contained picnic blankets. He made the sleeping man as comfortable and warm as he could, murmuring reassurances, then stepped quietly out of the building. Of course, Daniel couldn't bar the door behind him, but with no allies, supplies or communication lines, Curtis was running on luck now.

It wasn't the first time. It might be the last, but he'd give it a damned good try.

With that thought in mind, he took half a dozen steps before he heard the sound of movement, someone coming up the hill.

It was bare ground around the building and trying to hide behind the folly would look more suspicious than strolling forward. If it came to it, he'd just have to deal with the intruder as he'd dealt with Holt.

He paced forward as the walker approached, clenching and flexing his fingers, and saw it was Miss Merton.

"Hello, Mr. Curtis." She lifted a cheery hand as she came to meet him. "I thought I was the only morning walker here. Isn't it a beautiful day?" Her eyebrows drew together as she took in his appearance. "Are you all right?"

Curtis didn't hesitate. "Are you alone?"

"Yes...?"

"Miss Merton, in the name of God, as one shooter to another, I need your help."

Miss Merton straightened from Daniel's side and looked down at his unconscious form, then up at Curtis.

"Well, I don't think he's feverish, as such," she said. "Getting chilled through like that can do funny things to the body. You need to keep him warm and safe. I suppose you're certain of all this business?"

"As certain as I am of anything. I saw the photographs. He was tied to a rock—"

She held up a hand. "I don't doubt you. I'm just trying to think what to do."

"If you could help get food—"

"Not enough." Miss Merton shook her head briskly. "It seems to me that we have three problems: we must keep Mr. da Silva safe, get word out to someone for help, and avert suspicion until that help arrives. Very well. I think our first step should be to tell Fen."

"Miss Carruth?" said Curtis incredulously. Christ, had the woman not understood how serious this was?

She was giving him a pitying smile. "I suppose it's fair to say that there's rather more to Mr. da Silva than those ghastly affected airs he puts on?"

"Very much more."

"Well, you shouldn't be too quick to believe in Fen's silly-girl act either." She frowned in thought. "What if I announce I'm going for a tramp on the moors, alone, and beg supplies from the kitchen for the day. I'll bring a couple of guns and hole up here till evening. That way, I'll keep an eye on our invalid. You and Fen, somehow, will have to make that telephone call. You can relieve me in the evening. If the pair of you stay away from the folly in the day, nobody should even think of this place. Yes?"

No. Curtis didn't want to leave Daniel, not at all. He wanted to be the one standing guard. But if he didn't return, with Holt gone and Daniel missing from the cave, there would surely be a general alarm raised. And Miss Merton was competent and, so far as one could on such a short acquaintance, he trusted her.

"The Armstrongs are dangerous," Curtis warned her. "James especially, but they will all be desperate if they find out what we know, it's death to them. I don't imagine they'll hesitate to kill."

"Nor will I." Miss Merton sounded quite matter-of-fact. "I lost two brothers in the war. I feel quite strongly about treachery and selling secrets to our enemies. And I don't appreciate this blackmail business at all, and nor will Fen. Now, you wait here for me. I'll say I saw you out for a morning stroll and you'll doubtless be back for breakfast."

She left, striding out at a brisk pace. Curtis barred the door behind her and returned to Daniel's side.

He looked flushed, unkempt, and vulnerable, too, with his mouth open and no trace of the armour of mockery and affectation. Undefended, that was how he looked, and Curtis felt his fists tighten at the thought. If James Armstrong came by, he was looking forward to having it out with him.

The knock on the door, an hour or so later, was Miss Merton, in walking gear, with a very nice Holland and Holland shotgun under her arm and a knapsack, which she hefted. "Food and drink, and a revolver that I'll leave him. I'll see him right. Off you go, now. I've spoken to Fen."

"Be careful, won't you? And look after him. Thank you, Miss Merton."

"I'll look after him if you look after Fen," she said dryly. "And I think, under the circumstances, you may call me Pat."

Chapter Eleven

He was soon on "Fen" and "Archie" terms with Miss Carruth too. It felt comforting to have an ally at breakfast, as he explained how much better his knee was and she chattered artlessly about Pat's decision to go walking all day. Somehow, without the slightest impropriety, she managed to convey that now her companion's strict eye was lifted, she intended to have a little fun, and she accordingly attached herself to Curtis.

James Armstrong didn't seem to care. He was frowning at the table, noticeably depleted with the absence of Daniel, Holt and Pat Merton, and not long after they had finished the meal, when Fen was proposing a lazy stroll around the gardens, he came up to Curtis.

"I say, have you seen Holt?"

"I haven't, no. He's sleeping jolly late." Curtis let himself sound a touch disapproving.

"He's not in his room."

"Oh. Then he must have gone out early."

"Everyone seems to have done today," Fen put in. "Pat went off on one of her marches, and weren't you up early, Archie?"

"About six, I suppose. I can't say I saw Holt, though."

"Six!" Fen gave a tiny scream. "I need my beauty sleep."

"Then you must sleep a great deal," said Curtis, aware his role was to flirt a little, and also that he was really not very good at it.

Armstrong didn't come in to improve on that lumpen compliment. He seemed not to notice that Curtis had attracted the woman he'd been so doggedly pursuing. "I hope he shows up," he said, scowling. "You didn't hear anything last night?"

"Last night? When?"

"Any time."

Curtis shook his head. "I went to bed early, perhaps ten. Slept like a log, I'm afraid. You don't think Holt went out in the night? Why on earth would he do that?"

Armstrong was looking decidedly uncomfortable, and now Curtis was sure that he had known what Holt was up to. He had put Daniel in the cave, he'd known Holt was going back there in the night, for whatever hellish reason.

"I don't know," Armstrong said. "Maybe he heard a noise, or, or—"

"A burglar?" Fen gasped with horror. "You don't think he confronted a *burglar*?"

"Of course I don't, you st—you, you see." Armstrong's recovery was stumbling at best. Fen looked at him, pretty features setting into an expression of cold politeness, leaving him in no doubt she knew what he had almost said.

"I'm delighted to hear it, Mr. Armstrong. Come, Archie, escort me, please."

Curtis offered her his arm, and she swept out into the hall with an air of offended dignity that would have suited a dowager duchess. Armstrong didn't try to follow.

Once in the gardens, sure of privacy, Fen looked up at him, a laugh in her velvet-brown eyes. "Well! He wasn't very gracious, was he?"

"He's worried. Don't take this lightly, Miss—that is, Fen. I don't know how much Pat explained?"

"Everything I need to know, which is probably everything." Fen spoke with sublime confidence. "So Mr. Holt won't be coming back?"

"Ah— No. No, he won't."

"Good." He looked down at her, shocked. She made a face. "I thought he was quite nasty. He laughed at everyone, underneath. He was so polite to Sir Hubert, but one could see he was sneering really."

"Would you say so? I didn't notice."

"I did. I don't much like people who laugh up their sleeves."

"Da Silva's a little that way," Curtis observed ruefully.

"Do you think so?" Fen considered it. "I don't quite agree. That is, Mr. da Silva laughs at everyone, but he hopes someone else will get the joke too, don't you think?"

Curtis thought about that for a few moments, then said, "Yes. You're rather sharp."

Fen dimpled. "But Mr. Holt isn't like that. One was not supposed to get the joke, and if one did, it wasn't funny and it only made one feel worse."

"Was he offensive to you?"

"Oh, well." Fen paced forward, hands behind her back. "It's not that I mind flirting, you know. Mr. da Silva is the most dreadful flirt, and it's wonderfully amusing and desperately unserious. But Mr. Holt flirted rather horribly. Not in public, that was unremarkable, but alone. He *looked* at one so. One felt as though he knew things he shouldn't." She paused. "And I suppose he did, of course, with their spying. How utterly vile."

Curtis quelled his curiosity as to what Holt could have known about Fen. It was none of his business.

"Well, we've a chance to put an end to it," he observed. "We can have people up here to catch the brutes red-handed, if I can just make a telephone call without the operator eavesdropping."

"Yes, of course." Fen twinkled up at him. "I think I might be able to help you there."

They weren't able to act straightaway. First Lady Armstrong came out to meet them, giving them a roguish look and declaring that she had come to replace Miss Merton as chaperone. Fen went into peals of apparently unforced laughter at the weak witticism. Curtis, watching Lady Armstrong, saw strain in her eyes.

They were taken off to join the party. Most hostesses offered a relentless programme of entertainments for a country-house party; Lady Armstrong's popularity—and, in fact, the success of the blackmail venture—sprang from her willingness to allow guests to disappear off in twos during the day, as well as the general practice of arranging rooms to facilitate encounters at night.

Nevertheless, there was a certain level of appearance that had to be upheld. The guests of the reduced party, minus James, were gathered to try their hands at archery, since Sir Hubert had installed a range, and this was a sport enjoyed by both sexes. Curtis took part gamely. The bow would have been almost impossible for him to handle even if he'd been paying attention, which he was not, but at least he needed no excuse for his off-target shots.

After a couple of hours that might, under other circumstances, have flown by, they were led in for lunch. Curtis cursed Lady Armstrong's incessant fussing: when would the blasted woman let them alone? He was horribly aware of Daniel undefended, perhaps ill, perhaps worsening; Pat Merton, waiting alone—armed, but what if James Armstrong tracked her down? Would she have the nerve to shoot? And the clock was ticking. There would be very little chance of help arriving today, now, and the later he called, the longer it would take.

Curtis had been trapped by Boer forces in a South African *kraal*, lost behind enemy lines for two days without water, and treed by an enraged hippopotamus, which had been a great deal less amusing than it sounded. He didn't remember any of those times with fondness, but this house party was beginning to wear his nerves thinner than all of them.

"Do try the spiced beef, Mr. Curtis," Lady Armstrong said. "Cook makes it to a South African recipe, I believe."

"What do they eat in South Africa?" Mrs. Lambdon asked. "Zebras and things, I suppose?"

Curtis was dealing with that when the door opened and a rather hot-looking James Armstrong entered.

"You're late, boy," said Sir Hubert, with a frown.

"I'm sorry, pater, everyone. I went for a walk, lost track of time."

Curtis doubted that. He suspected James would have been up to the caves where he would have found—well, with luck, nothing. He would be wondering where Daniel was, where Holt was. He would, Curtis assumed, be aware that a bicycle was missing and thus that Holt had never come back from his trip.

Was he looking for Daniel? Did he have men out? In South Africa there were trackers, Bushmen who could follow spoor across miles of apparently featureless ground. The wizened, scrub-haired man that they had called King George would have been able to follow Curtis's tracks from the caves to the folly at a running pace, and would have known he was carrying another man too. Curtis hoped to hell that Peakholme's beaters didn't have those skills.

James settled at the table after another word of rebuke from his father. He looked distracted and concerned.

"I say," he remarked abruptly to Curtis. "I thought you were heading down south again, what?"

Curtis gave him a genial smile. "My rotten knee's rather better today, thank heavens. I mustn't be tempted by the long walks, but it's very well up to a stroll. That said—may I use your telephone to call my specialist?" he asked Lady Armstrong, seizing the opportunity. "Just to be sure."

"Of course. Whenever you like. The operator will be there till seven—you know we have our own operator for the system here?"

"I'd love to see how it works," Fen put in. "Daddy's firm built the system, you know, Archie. He'd be so disappointed if I didn't examine it. May I go and see your exchange? I don't understand a *thing* about wires, but I can tell him how wonderfully clever it looks."

"Of course, my dear." Lady Armstrong laughed at her, just a little, and the men all joined in. Fen smiled sweetly back.

They went down to the exchange after the interminable luncheon. Fen said, as they tramped the gravel paths, "I suppose you know lots of terribly rude words? From the army?"

"Er, some." Curtis was rather taken aback.

"Do feel free, then. In confidence, Pat uses some dreadful language—she grew up with four brothers, you know—and after a meal with those people, I'm rather missing her turn of phrase. I could *slap* Lady Armstrong, honestly." Fen looked ruffled and indignant. "For all they know Mr. da Silva is lying dead in a pit somewhere, and there she sits stuffing her face with cold chicken and rissoles. What a foul set they are."

"I couldn't agree more. What's your scheme for the exchange?"

"It depends on the operator. Follow my lead."

The telephone exchange was housed in an unobtrusive hut next to the generator, painted a dark green so as not to stand out from the woods that would one day surround it. A fast, narrow stream ran by the hut a little below them, turning a mill that provided part of the house's electric power.

Fen knocked on the door and smiled blindingly at the small, balding man who answered.

"Good afternoon, I'm Carruth. Fenella Carruth. My father, Peter Carruth, built the system for Sir Hubert."

The operator's face didn't change. He was apparently not a fanatic of the telephone. "Oh, aye, miss?"

"I've permission to see the exchange, you know. Sir Hubert *so* kindly said I could tell Daddy all about it." She tripped in, and Curtis followed, looking around with incomprehension at the board of wires and sockets. "Tell me, did he use the Repton transformers here?"

"Couldn't say, miss."

Fen nodded. "Well, Archie, do let me show you. To connect the call, you see, one has to connect a telephone to the switchboard. These are the front keys, here, for the house telephones. One places it in the jack, and then the back key connects to the other telephone. Now, do remind me." She radiated charm at the operator. "Which position connects the operator to the cord, and which is the ring generator?"

Curtis suspected that was the simplest question imaginable; it was certainly within the operator's power to answer. He beamed, and set forth the principle in exhaustive detail, prompted by Fen's artless questions, until just a few moments later she was seated at the desk, gurgling with laughter.

"So one simply connects this front key here, to this back key here, and then—now, Mr. Curtis, do give me the number of your medical specialist, and I shall be your operator!"

Curtis recited the number of his uncle's office. Fen, giggling at herself, put the call through, and said musically, "Calling for Mr. Archibald Curtis!" as soon as the call was answered, then leapt up, hand to mouth, as she handed the receiver over. "Oh but how rude, we can't eavesdrop on your medical matters." She clasped the operator's arm. "So *you* shall show me the generator, and we'll leave Mr. Curtis to his call."

The operator attempted a protest, but he had been taken by surprise, and there was, of course, nothing he could do unless he was to refuse a lady to her face. She hustled him out, and Curtis said into the receiver, to the questioning voice, "I must speak to Sir Maurice Vaizey. A matter of extreme urgency and national security. Get him now. A man's life is at stake."

Curtis came out of the hut a few moments later, and joined Fen and the operator in marvelling at the operation of the generator and the wonders of technological progress.

The operator looked awkward as they took their leave. "By rights, sir, miss, I oughtn't have left the equipment alone even for a minute."

"We've done no harm to it, I'm sure," Fen assured him.

"No, miss, but it's more than my job's worth."

"I dare say Sir Hubert would understand your courtesy," Curtis put in. "But if you'd prefer we didn't mention it to him...?"

"I'd be grateful, sir."

"Then at least, may I..." Curtis tipped him generously and took Fen's arm, and they strolled back to the house together in a mood of justified self-satisfaction.

Pat returned to the house not long before the dinner bell, in a flurry of cold air and red cheeks. Curtis had no opportunity to speak to her before she went up to change. It was unavoidable that they both had to be present at dinner. He only hoped that Daniel was in a state to watch over himself for a few hours, and was relieved to see James Armstrong at the dinner table too. He resolved to keep an eye on that young man throughout the evening.

"Where's Mr. Holt?" commented Pat, in a pause of the conversation. "Has he left us as well?"

"We're not quite sure," said Lady Armstrong. "He went out this morning for a bicycle ride, I understand, and he hasn't come back."

"Perhaps he got a puncture. The roads are awfully stony. I say, I wonder if it was him I saw."

"You saw him?" James's voice was sharp.

"I don't know if I saw him," Pat said patiently. "I saw a fellow who might have been him, on a bicycle, at about lunchtime, I suppose. I was having a bite to eat up that stony outcrop perhaps seven miles northeast of here."

"Oh, Pat, you are exhausting." Fen gave her an affectionate look. "So desperately healthy."

"But could it have been Holt?" James demanded.

"Miss Merton said, she doesn't know." Lady Armstrong's tone held a hint of command. "We've men out on the roads. There's nothing more to be done for now."

"It's almost certainly a puncture." Pat spoke with conviction. "I shouldn't bicycle here, I must say, one would be forever changing tires."

"Oh, you're a lady cyclist?" Mrs. Lambdon asked with some disapproval, and the conversation turned, to Curtis's relief, away from the man he had killed.

He managed a word with Pat before bed when the two women engineered the evening card tables so that the three of them were engaged in a game of Reunion. By this point Curtis had developed a respect for their organisational powers that verged on awe.

"He's not ill," Pat murmured. "He's got my revolver, and the door's locked. Bring water."

"Is he all right?" Curtis asked, as quietly as he could.

Pat gave him a look that struck as a little too sympathetic. "Highly strung. He'll do."

Fen took a trick with great glee at that point, and Curtis returned his attention to the game as best he could, which was to say that he was thoroughly trounced.

He waited with almost unbearable impatience for the party to break up that night. It was taking on a nightmarish aspect now he knew the masks these people wore. Sir Hubert's jovial manner seemed a parody of itself. James Armstrong and Lambdon struck him as not bluff but brutish, and Lady Armstrong's fluttering, affectionate ways were repulsive in their glaring falseness. He made himself smile and chat and play, and went to his room with fervent gratitude at the earliest opportunity.

Chapter Twelve

He waited till past midnight before slipping from the house, armed with a flask of water, a hip flask of whisky, a cold chicken pie pilfered from the kitchen, and a revolver. He took even more care than before, treading as lightly as he could to get over the gravel around the house, and keeping to the shadows of the trees, away from the drifts of autumn leaves, rain-sodden though they were. He was aware that the Armstrongs' men might still be out looking for Holt, and wished he had Daniel's stealth, but he encountered nobody on his cautious way up to the folly.

The door was locked. He knocked, softly, and then stood back, feeling very exposed, so that he was visible from the window. He hoped Daniel wasn't asleep.

There was the scrape of a heavy wooden bar, and the door opened.

Daniel stood in the doorway, rumpled, unshaven and disreputable in the baggy stolen garments, and Curtis's heart twisted at the sight. He hurried into the folly. Daniel barred the door behind him and turned.

Curtis had meant to ask at once whether Daniel had seen anything to suggest he'd been found, but the words had vanished from his mind. He was paralysed with the desire to take the man in his arms again, just to hold him close and feel his warmth.

"Curtis."

"Christ, I'm glad to see you," Curtis said with unthinking honesty.

"I'm glad to see you too. Not as glad as I was last time we met. But then, I never want to be quite so pathetically grateful to see anyone again." Daniel's voice sounded strong enough, but there was a twist of something nastily mocking in there.

Curtis tried to read his face in the darkness. "Are you all right?"

"Thanks to you. And the remarkable Miss Merton, of course. If James Armstrong had come along, I'm positive she'd have shot him on sight."

"I'm glad she didn't," Curtis said, matching Daniel's dry tone, because there was nothing of his own need in the other man's voice. *Control yourself, you damned fool.* "I've rather promised myself that I'll break his neck."

Daniel tilted his head, assessing. He was two feet away, and Curtis was vividly, physically aware of him, so close, not moving closer. "Have you? Yes, I believe you have. It would be better if you didn't."

"Why not?"

"We need to know what they've sold and to whom. Sir Hubert and Lady Armstrong are bright, Holt's dead. The egregious James is by far the most likely to talk, once in custody. You'll notice I'm assuming that you've managed to summon help."

"I spoke to Sir Maurice this afternoon. He's sending men up, to be here by the morning. We've just to wait it out now. For which purpose, I've a revolver, food and drink."

"Water, or actual drink?"

"Both."

"I do like you."

The tone was light enough, but the words hung in the air just a little too long. Curtis stared at the dark shape, wishing he could see better.

"Come up here, it's less uncomfortable." Daniel led the way up the winding stair to the mezzanine, where the mullioned windows let in what moonlight there was. "What's happened about Holt?"

"He's been missed, of course. James is suspicious of something, though Pat made a good effort to throw him off the track. I don't think they're panicking yet."

"And with luck, our relief will have arrived before they start tomorrow." The picnic blankets were piled on the wooden floor. Daniel waved a hand in the manner of a gracious host, and they seated themselves, side by side, backs against the stone wall. It was cold, but not unbearably so. Curtis passed over food and water.

"Thanks." Daniel took a bite of pie. "Tell me. How did you know I was there, in the cave?"

"Well, I couldn't see how you'd have upped sticks with all your things. The Armstrongs claimed you'd been asked to leave for cheating at cards with Holt and Armstrong—"

"If I had cheated that pair at cards, you would know about it because they'd both be wandering around in their drawers, having lost the shirts off their backs."

"I *thought* you'd be able to fuzz cards." Curtis felt obscurely proud of his colleague's accomplishments.

"I can; I didn't. Go on."

Curtis explained about Armstrong's remark and the inference he'd drawn. Daniel turned and stared at him. He shifted uncomfortably. "What?"

"You walked two miles to explore a cave in the middle of the night, based on a chance remark of that insupportable cretin Armstrong?"

"It was the only idea I had. I couldn't think what else to do."

"I'm not arguing, I'm marvelling at my own good fortune. Listen, Curtis, I can't tell you how grateful I am—"

"Don't. No, really, you thanked me quite enough last night." That wasn't true, as such, but he had no need for gratitude, and he couldn't bear that tremor of anger and shame in Daniel's voice. "It was no more than any decent man would have done under the circumstances, and you'd have done the same for me."

"I hate to disabuse you, my dear fellow, but I wouldn't do it for my own mother. I'm an utter coward about being underground. And have learned a valuable lesson about keeping that fact to myself."

"I knew a fellow with a dreadful fear of spiders," Curtis offered. "In the army. Big chap, near my size, tough as old boots, and terrified of a little spider, poor chap."

"And doubtless you all ridiculed him for it without mercy. I'm well aware it's irrational, and cowardly, and whatever you like. I just—feel the earth above me, that's all. I can feel the entire weight of it, millions of tons, millions of years, pressing down on my head—"

Curtis put a hand on his shoulder, stopping him. "Do you know what a sergeant told me before I went into battle for the first time?"

"No?"

"He said his best advice was to get to the latrines in good time, because a good few of us were going to soil ourselves in terror." Daniel twisted round to look at him, and Curtis grinned at his expression. "What I mean is, one can't help one's fears. The question isn't if you're a fellow who cries in the night before a big engagement—and I knew a damned brave man who did exactly that, regularly. It's whether you pick yourself up the next day."

"What was your rank?" Daniel asked.

"Captain."

"Really. I'm astonished you weren't a general."

That was waspish, but more the Daniel he knew. After a second, Daniel leaned against him, and Curtis shifted his arm around his neck, just to make them both more comfortable.

"Were you afraid?" Daniel asked abruptly. "In battle?"

"Not much. I've very little imagination. It's the imaginative chaps who suffer."

"'The coward dies a thousand deaths'?"

Curtis shook his head. "These chaps put themselves at risk for their country. Cowards don't do that."

Daniel was silent for a few moments, but Curtis was sure his body had lost some of its tension. He watched the back of his dark head, the nape of his neck. He wanted, so much, to lean forward, to touch that skin with his lips, the lightest brush.

He asked, "What happened, anyway? How did they catch you?"

"Oh, rotten luck. I let myself into the service corridor while everyone was downstairs—I thought it was most likely to be unoccupied then. Unfortunately, that brute March came along with a couple of his pals, and he summoned Holt. I had no chance of talking my way out of it to that pair, and from inside the corridor, it's impossible not to see what they're up to, with the cameras and mirrors." Daniel shifted his weight closer against Curtis. "And of course Holt doesn't like me, what with my irritating habit of Judaism, and that stupid showy performance at billiards, from which I really could have refrained." He sighed. "I have *not* covered myself in glory on this mission."

Curtis tightened his arm. "So what happened then?"

"Well, Holt wanted to know how I got in there. Whether you knew what I was doing. I went all whiny East End in an effort to persuade him I was just an opportunistic thief, but he chose not to believe me. Which was when he came up with the bright idea of the cave." Curtis felt his convulsive swallow. "The idea being, you see, that after a day underground I should be ready to tell them whatever they wanted, which was of course quite correct, except that it didn't take anything like a day, not with that bloody water dripping down like stones falling and the c-cold—" He stopped short, then took a deep breath, exhaled hard, and went on with just the barest tremor in his voice. "Holt was too clever for his own good. I don't honestly think he believed I was more than a thief. I think he wanted to find a reason to torture me. Or even, to torture *somebody*, and I happened to be in a vulnerable position."

"I'm damned sorry I gave him the idea with that blasted story."

"I'm not. For one thing, I shouldn't have preferred it if he'd used knives or needles. For another, it's thanks to his desire to see me go mad underground that you were able to reach me, for which—"

"Sssh." Curtis pulled him closer and felt Daniel twist to slip his arms round his chest.

They held each other in silence, in the chilly dark, with the faint light of the moon through the mullioned window casting everything grey. Curtis found, to his own slight surprise, that he was stroking Daniel's hair. Daniel wasn't objecting.

"Holt," Daniel said at last. "You killed him."

Curtis's hand stopped briefly. "Yes."

"I was in something of a state at the time, what with the cold, and spending a day in an utter funk, and I'll admit I wasn't entirely in my right mind. Nevertheless, it did seem to me that neither were you."

"No." Curtis had no idea what else to say about that.

"Was that what they call a berserk state?"

"You've read that damned book about my uncle, haven't you?"

"Well, I have, but I have also read a number of Icelandic sagas," said Daniel astonishingly. "I did my master's thesis on Old Norse."

"You've an MA?" said Curtis, with the instinctive alarm of one who had got a place at Oxford on the strength of his boxing.

"The German equivalent, as it happens, from Heidelberg. Hence I have read a fair few descriptions of berserk warriors, and I must say, Curtis... You looked about twice your already substantial size, you kept laughing, which was unnerving, and of course you broke his neck with your bare hands. It was a sight to behold. I don't speak in a spirit of criticism, I was just rather startled," he added. "Much as if one had come across a Roman legionary, alive and well in the twentieth century."

Curtis shrugged uncomfortably. "I don't know what to tell you. Quatermain, the writer fellow, used to say my uncle and I are throwbacks to our Norse forefathers. Race memory or some such tripe. Nonsense, if you ask me. I lose control of myself in a scrap sometimes, that's all. I don't much like it."

"No, I don't suppose you do. Did Holt get you with that knife?"

Curtis appreciated the absence of sympathy or apology in the deft shift of subject. It was one of the things that made Daniel so easy to talk to, at least when he wasn't in one of his prickly moods. "Slashed my forearm. It's not deep. My coat took the brunt." He had bundled the ripped coat up with his blood-soaked shirt and hidden them in the wardrobe, then closed the wound with strips of sticking plaster. It wasn't comfortable, but it would heal.

"A bit low, that, pulling a knife. He was, of course, terrified of you and about to die, but still." Daniel shook his head and said, with some satisfaction, and in a creditable impression of Holt's tones, "Damned dirty dago trick."

"That's what I thought!" Curtis exclaimed, and felt Daniel shake with silent laughter against him. They were more or less reclining against one another now, Curtis on his back and Daniel on his side, which would have been pleasant if Curtis's spine hadn't been objecting so strenuously.

"I need to sit up," he said with regret.

Daniel rolled away. Curtis had no idea what to say to bring him back. He sat up, legs apart with knees bent, and managed, "It's jolly cold."

"Should we huddle together for warmth?" enquired Daniel, moving as he spoke to position himself with his back to Curtis, leaning on his chest, seated between his legs. Curtis, heart beating a little too strongly, draped his arms over Daniel's shoulders, and allowed himself to luxuriate in the closeness.

"Why did you go to Heidelberg for your MA?" he asked, for something to say. "I mean, why Germany?"

"Various reasons," Daniel said, and after a moment, "I was kicked out of Cambridge."

"Oh." That was something of a facer. "For your, er, personal life?"

"In its way." Daniel tilted his head back. "There was a young Adonis from the boating crew. One of the golden lads, you know. Clean-limbed noble English youth. The stuff that dreams are made on, for a ragamuffin from the East End. I was utterly besotted, and he—returned my interest, and there was one charmed, sun-drenched Easter term, and then we were caught in the boathouse by the rowing crew. And then there was the talk, the whispers. So my beloved decided to explain things away by going to the Dean to accuse me of indecent assault."

"What?"

"Oh, he'd reasoned it all out." Daniel didn't look round. "He was the second son of a duke, you see, he had a social position to lose. Whereas my father's a Spitalfields locksmith, my entire family had had to scrape together the pennies to fund my place at Cambridge. He *belonged* there. I didn't. And thus, I had far less to lose than he did by being thrown out in disgrace. He was quite sure of that."

Curtis swallowed. He found it hard to keep his voice level. "Christ, Daniel. That's..." He tailed off, lost for words.

"It was fairly bad," Daniel said. "Of course, the Dean knew it was so much hot air, but he took the same view as my erstwhile lover on our relative importance. At least he was sufficiently embarrassed to seal the records on the incident, so it didn't blight my career quite so much as it might have. As it happens, I took a full scholarship to Heidelberg not long afterwards, which put paid to the family recriminations, so from that perspective it was doubtless for the best. I should probably have thanked him."

"The selfish shitlouse."

"It did him no good. He was arrested two years later—pure chance, a police raid on a Cleveland Street molly house, he was just one of many picked up. He shot himself after he was released."

"Oh God." Curtis had no idea what to say to a story like that. He'd heard so often that "men like that should shoot themselves". This was the first time it had struck home that they did.

"Yes." Daniel was silent a moment. "Well. Enough of that. I don't know why I bored you with that unedifying tale."

"I'm glad you told me." Curtis frowned, thinking about it. "You are careful, aren't you? That is, might you not find yourself in trouble too?"

Daniel paused for a second. "By *trouble*, do you mean spending a day tied to a rock waiting to be murdered?"

"No, I mean with the police."

"Yes, my dear, I know, I'm just amazed by your perspective on life. In fact, I am very cautious, little though you may think it."

Curtis didn't think it at all, and he found himself seized with alarm at this threat to Daniel, which he had somehow never considered before. "You're nothing of the kind," he objected. "You make it very plain—"

"I may do, but that's not illegal. One has to be caught in the act, as it were, they don't arrest one for being campish quite yet. Really, don't worry. I know what I'm about."

That was more than Curtis did, and Daniel's light tone had a hint of steel that warned him to drop the subject. "Well, if you say so." He ran his hand down the crumpled linen instead, smoothing it over the warm skin beneath. "So how did you come to work for my uncle? You, er, don't strike me as the type."

"My dear chap, I open locks, move quietly, have few qualms about gentlemanly behaviour, and speak the language of one of our major European rivals. I'm precisely the type, and there are people who keep their eyes open for such things."

"Even with the, er..."

"Especially with the 'er'. Your revered uncle told me once that he found it convenient to have a few queers he could call on when necessary. I assured him I felt the same."

"You did not."

"I did. He didn't laugh."

"I'll bet he didn't," said Curtis faintly, considering his formidable uncle. "You've nerve."

His hand was running up and down Daniel's torso, further each time. It felt like an inestimable privilege to sit here, in the dark, touching him. He let his fingers spread and they met something oddly solid. He felt it, not really thinking what he was doing, noted that it was small, round and hard, and realised that he was fondling the nipple ring just as Daniel gave a distinctly inviting purr.

"Oh," he said, and carefully touched it again, giving it the slightest rub this time.

"Mmm." Daniel's back arched, pushing towards Curtis's hand. He ran a thumb firmly over the little nub. "*Mmm.*"

"Is it—that is, may I—" He had no idea what he was asking, but Daniel said, throatily, "You may," and reached up to flick open a couple of buttons. Curtis slid his hand inside the opened shirt, over Daniel's smooth, warm skin. His fingers made direct contact with the silver ring and the erect nipple it pierced, and both of them jolted at the touch. Curtis rubbed with finger and thumb, not sure what he was doing, but thrillingly aware of the effect he was having on the other man. Daniel's breathing was deepening, he was shifting under Curtis's hand, and perhaps it was the shadows of the faint moonlight, but...

Curtis cursed his own mutilated state, but at least the glove concealed his ugly deformity, even if it cut off so much sensation. He leaned forward, still caressing Daniel's chest with his left hand, and brushed the right over Daniel's waist and further down.

Yes: Daniel was very definitely excited by what he was doing.

He began to stroke there too, through the dark material, running his hand over the hard arousal. Daniel made a whimpering noise, bucking his hips forward in invitation, and Curtis realised that his two-digit grip would be no use at all for what he wanted to do.

"Hold on," he murmured, giving Daniel's nipple a little pinch and eliciting a gasp of pleasure that went straight to his own groin. "Let me just—" He transferred his working hand down to Daniel's waist, and moved the gloved right hand up to his nipple.

Daniel shook his head at the touch of leather. "Take it off."

"What?"

"The glove."

"It's not a pretty sight."

"I don't want your aesthetic judgement," Daniel bit out. "I want your *skin*."

Curtis hesitated, but it was dark, and he wanted to touch, so much. He pulled the leather off and dropped it to one side. The gnarled scar tissue was black in the dim light. Daniel's elegant hand met his own mutilation, his fingers closed round Curtis's scars, and then he guided the hand back down to his nipple.

And after all, finger and thumb were all Curtis needed for that.

He dealt with the trouser buttons, remembering with a shock as the hard cock sprang to his hand that of course the man had no drawers after that hellish night, and wrapped his good hand around Daniel's erection. It was in proportion to the rest of him, long and slender and smooth, and he caressed it, up and down, as he worked the tight nipple and felt Daniel buck against him with an ecstasy that Curtis could hardly believe he'd created.

"Daniel," he whispered.

Daniel's head was thrown back, eyes shut, mouth open, spine arched. He was thrusting gently into Curtis's hand, but allowing him to set the pace. Curtis realised that he was in control of Daniel's responsive, willing body now, and the thought made his own cock throb almost unbearably. "Oh God, Daniel. I should have done this before. I wanted to." And there was something else he'd wanted to do. He shifted and twisted down, keeping his hands working as best he could, till he could press his face to Daniel's chest. So smooth, so warm, a tang of salt sweat on his lips. He found Daniel's other nipple with his mouth and kissed it.

"You *should* have done this before." Daniel gave a grunt as Curtis sucked, then licked, amazed at his own daring. "We should have done nothing else all week. Oh, yes, like that. *That.*"

"I wanted to touch you." Curtis whispered the words, not sure if Daniel could hear, or was even listening. His hips were moving faster and his cock was so hard in Curtis's hand now. "I wanted to touch you all the time. Back in my room, with that collar stud, I thought you were going to bring me off just by talking—"

Daniel gasped a laugh. "I will. Some day."

"I want to bring you off. I want you to come because of me."

Daniel twisted under his fingers, back arching, for once beyond speech. Curtis tightened his grip on the nipple, pinching, and gave a triumphant grunt as Daniel gasped and thrashed and jerked with climax, spilling over Holt's stolen shirt, and his own bare chest, and finally Curtis's fingers, as he milked the last few drops till he heard the whimper of oversensitivity.

Daniel slumped against him, boneless. Curtis bit his lip against his own arousal, enjoying this moment. He felt like a conquering hero, and Daniel, tousled and spent, looked entirely conquered.

"What are you grinning at?" Daniel asked, without opening his eyes.

"Nothing." Curtis looked at the almost hairless chest, the dark nipples. "Why do you only have one of them pierced?"

"If you could do that to me with both tits, I'd never get out of bed again."

Curtis had to laugh. Daniel's mouth curved responsively. Curtis carefully cleaned him off as best he could with his handkerchief, straightened up his clothing, and tugged him up and closer, pulling a heavy, scratchy blanket over them both.

"Let me—" Daniel began.

"No, stay there." He owed Daniel this pleasure. And he would not have another chance to hold him in his arms all night. That had seemed inevitable two days ago; last evening he'd have been pathetically grateful to know he was alive; now it felt unbearable that it had to end so soon. He held on to him, keeping him warm and safe and close.

Daniel's hands were tracing shapes on his legs. He spoke after a few moments. "Tell me, how did you get me back from the cave?"

"Carried you. Why?"

"The small matter of your injured knee, that's all." Daniel sat up. "Good God, Curtis, I was hoping you'd say you had a bicycle, or a cart, or a native bearer. Have you damaged yourself?"

"Not at all. It feels better than it has since Jacobsdal. I'm serious," he insisted as Daniel twisted round to give him a look of incredulity. "My doctors have told me for months now there's no permanent damage done, no reason for the pain, and that exercise was all it needed, and perhaps they were right. It's been better since I came here, in fact. I wouldn't have described this as a rest cure, but it seems to have worked, all the same."

"Really?" Daniel reclined again. "Hmm."

"What?"

"I met a chap in Vienna, an up-and-coming young doctor, who had some interesting ideas on this sort of thing. He'd probably tell you that your mind created the pain, and took it away again."

"What? Why would it do that?"

"The idea is that your unconscious mind—you know what that is?—operates on the body. So, for example, you might have felt guilty about not fighting as a soldier any more, so your body acted as though it was wounded, creating the pain to justify you being out of action. Then once you were recalled to active service, as it were, you no longer needed to inflict the injury on yourself and the pain went away. Something along those lines."

"What absolute hogwash. Why on earth would one do such a thing to oneself? How?"

"It's unconscious, that's the point. Look, that African magic one reads about, when an unfortunate is placed under a curse and pines away. Does that happen?"

"It does, yes. My uncle saw it a few times."

"Is that magic at work?"

"No, of course not. The victims are persuaded they're going to die, so they do."

"Exactly. The unconscious mind affects the body. Isn't that the same thing?"

"But that's native superstition," Curtis protested. "I'm an educated Englishman."

"With a much less painful knee."

"Yes, but... No, really, it's nonsense."

Daniel shrugged. "Well, I don't know. It's a new theory, but the doctor struck me as a very bright man. That said, I actually went to see him about my fear of the underground, since he's already achieved some remarkable results with phobias, and he told me it was undoubtedly related to my homosexuality, so judge for yourself."

Curtis blinked. "To your...?"

"Homosexuality. Inversion. Attraction to one's own sex, dear heart. You must read Krafft-Ebing."

Curtis had no idea what that was, and suspected that he would rather not find out. He struck back to the point at issue. "This quack said you're afraid of caves because you're inverted?"

"Such was his theory, yes."

Curtis had no trouble spotting the logical flaw in that bit of claptrap. "Well, that doesn't hold water. *I'm* not afraid of—" He stopped dead.

There was an electric silence for a few seconds, then Daniel spoke, tone light and casual. "Thus, we have a hypothesis to test. How many times must one toss a chap off before a cellar paralyses one with terror? Feel free to research the theory in depth." He batted his eyelids absurdly.

"You do talk a lot of nonsense." Curtis brushed a grateful hand over Daniel's fingers.

"Don't blame me, blame the Viennese doctor." Daniel paused. "He did have fascinating opinions, though. Do you know what he said came between fear and sex?"

That sounded like it was going to be another of those appalling modern ideas. Curtis asked, cautiously, "What?"

"*Funf.*"

It was a ridiculous schoolboy joke, one that he'd heard cracked a dozen times at Eton as they'd learned to count in German. It was also the last thing in the world he'd expected to hear from Daniel at this moment, and Curtis doubled over with laughter, not so much at the absurd pun as at the ease with which he'd been caught. Against him, Daniel was shaking with amusement too, and Curtis held him and laughed till tears ran down his face, in a way he hadn't done since Jacobsdal, in this little safe place outside the world.

Chapter Thirteen

They sat in silence for a few moments after the laughing fit had passed, sharing the whisky. Daniel took a swig from the hip flask and passed it over. "Ought you sleep?"

"I'll watch. You sleep."

"I slept all day. I'll wake you in the event of trouble. Are we anticipating any?"

"I don't see why we should be. Sir Maurice told me to expect reinforcements early in the morning. I'll go back in, I suppose, and try to keep things looking normal."

"Good. The trick will be to stop them destroying the evidence when they realise they've been rumbled. Vaizey will want to know who's been up to what, and for that, he'll want the files."

"About that," Curtis said reluctantly.

"Ye-es. I've failed to remove any photographs of us to date, of course. That needs to be done. I don't think going in tonight—"

"Out of the question."

"Then we shall just have to deal with it tomorrow. Leave that to me, if you would." Daniel hesitated. "Look, the worst that will happen is that the Armstrongs will get those photographs into the hands of Vaizey, or his men and thence to him. Whatever he might think, he won't allow them, or word of them, to go further. He's good at keeping matters quiet."

"I don't much want him to have them, though." That was understating things. Sir Maurice was possessed of a cold, ferocious temper and a force of personality that would probably still reduce Curtis to a stammering schoolboy when he was fifty. More than that, he and Sir Henry were Curtis's family, the closest thing he had to parents. They could not be allowed to know of this. He could not believe that he was doing anything wrong in lying here with Daniel, not when it felt so simple and so comfortable, but he had no intention whatsoever of trying to make his uncles understand that, and to disappoint them was not thinkable.

"Obviously not," Daniel said. "And I'll try to avoid it. But if it comes to that, let me handle him. If I tell him the situation was forced on you—"

"No," said Curtis, with emphasis.

"Then I'll claim we were posing. Or something. Just let me deal with it, hmm?"

"I'm not having you shoulder the blame for this."

"I don't propose to shoulder it, I propose to shift it firmly onto the Armstrongs where it belongs. I bow to your experience in matters of physical violence, my dear Viking. I do wish you'd leave the low cunning to me."

"Your what?" demanded Curtis.

Daniel rolled sideways so that he could run a hand over Curtis's chest, slipping a finger between buttons into the coarse hair. "Viking," he said. "Huge, muscular, rampant—"

"Oh my God, don't start that again."

Daniel's eyes were dark stars, their gaze darting up from under lazily hooded eyelids. "A great, powerful brute of a man, bent on rape and pillage—"

"Good heavens!" Curtis exclaimed, half-laughing, rather shocked. "One wouldn't believe you're a poet." He paused. "You are, aren't you? That is, you did write those poems? It's not part of your pretence?"

"Of course I bloody did." A distinct note of the East End rang in the vowels of that offended response. "Who'd you think wrote them, Gladstone?"

Curtis grinned down at him, absurdly charmed by that tiny chink in his armour. "I didn't think anyone else could have written them. They're just like you." Daniel cocked a wary, questioning eyebrow. "Incomprehensible," Curtis told him, "and far too clever for their own good, and hiding all sorts of things, and—rather beautiful."

Daniel's mouth opened. He didn't respond for a second, then he sat up, twisted round to face Curtis, took his jaw in both hands, pulled him over and kissed him.

His mouth was soft and tender, and open, tongue darting against Curtis's lips, and Curtis, amazed and electrified, moved his own tongue tentatively, at first, then more strongly, delighting in the taste, the freedom to explore, in having this at last. It was gentle for a moment, until he felt rather than heard Daniel's tiny murmur against his mouth and one or both of them started making the kiss harder. Curtis felt Daniel's hands move over his shoulders and put his own hands on the slender back, and then, with sudden need, pulled him close. Daniel was in his arms now, curving against him, and he was kissing the man so fiercely that he could feel his teeth grinding against his own lips. His mouth was hot and desperate and his hands were clutching Curtis's hair, and Curtis gave up thinking and concentrated on the sensation of stubble against his skin, the mouth devouring his own with painful hunger, and the slender body wrapping itself around his as though Daniel wanted to press himself inside Curtis's skin.

Gradually the kiss grew less frantic again, but the need underneath it had built to a point of urgency. Curtis ran his hands over Daniel's hair and face, careful not to scrape scar tissue against softer flesh, and down and under his jacket. Daniel's hands were on his own shirt buttons, and Curtis felt the cold air as the linen was pushed back. Somehow they managed to get the layers of impeding clothing undone without entirely breaking the kiss, though Daniel cursed against Curtis's lips as he struggled with a cuff, until they were clinging together, chest to chest, mouth to mouth.

Curtis pulled back to look at Daniel. His jaw was shaded dark with stubble, hair tousled, that irresistible nipple ring winking bright in the shadowy room, and he was watching Curtis with something like awe.

"Look at you." Daniel traced a fingertip around the bulky pectorals, over the thick abdominal muscles, up Curtis's uninjured arm, and back over his broad shoulders. "You *are* a Viking."

"What does that make you?"

"The wrong side of Europe."

Daniel's fingertips brushed Curtis's nipples. He stiffened, not quite sure if he liked that, and with his usual quick understanding, Daniel ran his fingers away. They headed down, instead, and Curtis felt the buttons at his waist give. He reached for Daniel's waistband at the same time, and as he manipulated the fastenings one-handed, Daniel shifted forward and claimed his mouth again. Then they were kissing hard once more, rocking back and forth, Curtis's big powerful hand wrapped round both cocks, holding them together. Daniel grunted and went backwards, pulling Curtis down on top of him so that they lay on the nest of blankets, entwined and still half-clothed, thrusting against each other with increasing urgency. Daniel was hard and hot in Curtis's hand, moaning into his mouth, and now it was all about the bewildering pleasure of Daniel's abandoned writhing, the smooth body under him, most of all the warm, mobile lips open against his own. He was kissing Daniel when he came.

He rocked back and forth with the last shudders of orgasm, holding himself tight against Daniel, hand wet and slippery.

Daniel was taking longer, and as soon as he had his breath back, Curtis shifted position, still working him with his hand, and brought his mouth to Daniel's nipple, eliciting what could only be called a squeal. That was good, but he wanted, needed more. He wanted to make Daniel come apart, wanted to do what he should have done days ago, so he gathered up his courage and headed south.

"Curtis," gasped Daniel as he tentatively licked his cock. It was very smooth, and wet, and tasted musky and—well, that must be the taste of spunk, of course. It was slippery, and more astringent than he'd have thought, but not unpleasant. He moved his mouth over the head, unsure of what he was doing, but gaining confidence from Daniel's quivering stiffness.

"God. Are you sure—don't—"

"I want to," Curtis mumbled, and tried moving his head up and down, as Daniel had done to him.

"Oh sweet heaven mother fuck." Daniel's hips were jerking. "*Fuck.* Curtis—"

Curtis pulled his mouth away. "Archie."

"Archie." It was almost reverent.

Curtis concentrated on Daniel then, his taste, the shape of him in his mouth, the glorious noises of pleasure he made. He could feel his own body stirring again as he sucked and licked. He'd always assumed the act would be unpleasant, at best a service or a chore. He hadn't realised how much one might want to give someone that gift, how astonishing it was to feel the jerks and twitches, hear the whimpers, know one had caused them. He hadn't understood that sucking off a man was not at all the same thing as making love to Daniel.

A hand tightened in his hair. "Get out of the way," Daniel said urgently.

Curtis took the warning—next time he wouldn't, he told himself—and withdrew Daniel's cock from his mouth, then dared to lick at it again, outlining the smooth head, tasting the fluid beading there.

"Archie," whispered Daniel, and jerked against his hand.

"Daniel. Now, please, now." Curtis choked out the words as if he were climaxing himself, and gasped as he watched the white spatter hit Daniel's skin. He could feel the taste in his mouth.

Daniel lay, chest heaving. Curtis licked his lips and reached for the whisky.

"Well might you drink. Ah...have you done that before?"

"No." Curtis found himself somewhat embarrassed by his own inexperience, which was absurd. The fact was, there were the men who did that to other men, and there were the men to whom it was done, and Curtis had always been in the latter group. It had never seemed expected that he would reciprocate, not with his mouth, and he had never offered. Well, he wouldn't. He wasn't that sort of chap.

The thought caught him sharply for a second, but Daniel was looking at him with startled pleasure, and Curtis found himself tugged down for a deep kiss that drove everything from his mind but the sweep of tongues and the movement of lips. Daniel seemed not to object to the taste of himself in Curtis's mouth.

After a breathless moment, Daniel released him. "Which is to indicate that I'm honoured, my dear."

"What? Oh, nonsense." Curtis grabbed for the now rather soiled handkerchief and made an effort at cleaning them both up.

Daniel waved a hand. "I'm filthy anyway, don't worry."

They managed to get into some kind of comfort again, snuggled together on the hard floor under scratchy, musty blankets. Curtis ran his hand over Daniel's stubbled jawline and leaned forward to kiss him, because he could.

"This is the most peculiar house party of my experience."

Daniel chuckled, then nuzzled into Curtis's chest. "It's had its moments."

Curtis looked down at the dark head, felt those clever, exploratory fingers running over his muscles and said, without planning, "May I call on you?"

Daniel's fingers stilled. "Sorry?"

"In London. When this business is done with. May I call on you?"

"*Call* on me?"

He sounded incredulous. Curtis felt himself redden. "Or however one should put it."

"Ah." Daniel relaxed perceptibly. "If you mean, may you visit for a fuck, then, my dear fellow—"

"No," Curtis said strongly, and then, "Well, that is, yes. If you'd like to. But that's not what I meant."

"Then what did you mean?" Daniel had a frown between his eyes, as if the commonplace phrase had made no sense to him.

"I don't know how else to say it. I don't know how men conduct these things between themselves. If I liked and respected a lady, I'd ask permission to call—"

"I'm not a lady. I wouldn't be a lady even if I were a woman."

Curtis sighed. "Good Lord, help a fellow out here."

"I don't know what you want."

How they had managed to lose that instant, easy understanding? "It seems quite straightforward to me."

"Unfortunately, my dear, you are so straightforward I sometimes have trouble understanding a word you say."

Daniel's tone was very smooth and mannered, and Curtis fought an urge to say, "Never mind" and retreat. He set his shoulders against the real possibility that he was about to make a hopeless fool of himself. He hadn't thought this through in the slightest, but he knew the truth of his own words as he spoke. "I mean, I want to see you again. Spend time with you. This, of course"—he waved a hand at their entwined bodies— "but...more. Damn it, Daniel, I want to be with you. You're brave and clever and rather wonderful, and I even like your poems, and—"

"Stop!" It was almost a shout. "Stop, stop, *stop.*"

Curtis stared down. Daniel looked up at him with troubled eyes. His shoulders were hunching.

"What on earth—"

"Don't say those things."

"Why not?"

Daniel shut his eyes. "Because that is what gentlemen do, and I am—not a gentleman. I'm sure we will fuck like the songs of angels, and I look forward to it. But no more than that, hmm?"

"I don't understand."

Daniel opened his eyes again to shoot him a glare. "My father is a Spitalfields locksmith. I was brought up between his shop and my uncle's billiard hall, which my mother manages in a very low-cut dress. I learned to mimic my betters from another uncle who recites Shakespeare in the superior sort of music hall. I dress well because *another* uncle is a tailor of excellent imitative powers, not because I can afford a decent suit of clothes. I'm the only one in my grotesquely extensive family who's ever been to university. You know damned well I'm not of your class."

"What has that to do with anything?"

"Everything."

Curtis wasn't sure what to reply to that. "All I'm saying is, I don't want to treat you like a...whatever the equivalent of a mistress might be." Curtis reached out tentatively to touch him. Daniel didn't pull away, but he didn't respond either. "Look, if it's that you don't want to see me in London, for God's sake say so. I don't mean to be a nuisance."

"It's not that." Daniel let out a long sigh. "Oh, for— Listen, Curtis."

"I wish you'd call me Archie."

"This has been the devil of a week, and you've come to some rather rapid conclusions. I suspect that when you return to London this will all seem like a nightmare, or an aberration, or at the least a very poor idea."

"Daniel—"

"I'm still talking."

"Of course you are."

Daniel gave the barest twitch of a smile. "The thing is, you are a gentleman. In the true meaning of the word. I don't want you to feel bound by anything you've said, or to resent me because you shouldn't have said it. I don't want you to put yourself in a corner. And I won't be blamed for it if you do."

Curtis said, with some force, "I am not your bloody duke."

"Son of a duke."

"More like son of a—" Curtis stopped himself, remembering the fellow was dead. "That is, don't assume I'll behave like a cad."

"I don't want you to behave like a gentleman. Not if it means honouring a commitment you shouldn't have made. You're not in the habit of going back on your word, are you?"

"No, and I don't change my mind a great deal, either."

"You seem to have changed it about what you want recently," Daniel pointed out. "You might wish to change it back."

That's my affair, Curtis wanted to say, but of course it wasn't only his, not if Daniel cared what he felt. Not if Daniel was afraid to let him come close for fear of being pushed away.

"You're not the first man I've been with," he said abruptly. "I've done plenty of things before. I've never found a woman I felt fond of, in that way. Damn it, I've never kissed a woman of my own class."

Daniel blinked. "You're not serious."

He was. He'd had a few unsatisfactory encounters with ladies for hire, but had never felt the urge to pursue a flirtation that would lead to commitment. *Waiting for the right woman*, he'd told his uncles, but he'd been quite content to wait, because the prospect of marriage had seemed as dry and joyless as the rest of his future. "I haven't changed my mind about myself. I've just—failed to consider matters until now. I never had to, in the army." He paused, then said, with more difficulty than he'd expected, "I had someone. My lieutenant."

"He was your lover?"

"Oh—well..." The word sounded extraordinary in the context of George Fisher. He'd been a redheaded sunburnt fellow, a comrade in arms, a friend. "He was my tentmate. We used to, you know. This sort of thing."

"May I suggest you use verbs and nouns? They won't change what happened, and you might even become more accustomed to things." Daniel sounded, not entirely unsympathetic, but a little dry. "I'm not asking you to speak about private matters, but if you *are* going to speak about them, do use words."

Curtis gritted his teeth. "All right, if you must. We tossed each other off sometimes, and it wasn't something we discussed, just something we did. He didn't talk all the damned time, and I never really thought about it, what with being rather busy with the Boers. He wasn't my lover. It wasn't like that." Curtis had never kissed Fisher, never felt the urge. He wondered if Fisher might have wanted him to. "But he was my friend, my companion, and he died when the Lafayette gun I'd given him exploded. He bled to death while I watched—" He stopped, the lump in his throat choking him.

Daniel's fingers closed on Curtis's right hand, over the scarred knuckles. "I'm sorry." He said nothing else, and Curtis breathed out evenly, over the tightness in his lungs.

"Anyway. That was how things were out in South Africa. And it hasn't been an issue since then. The last year or so has been..." *A living death*, he wanted to say, but that was hardly fair on Daniel. "Tiresome. It's been a long time since I've felt that I wanted anything, from anyone. But when I did, now I look at it, it's always been with men. Nothing's changed. You must think I'm a bloody fool."

"That's not what I was thinking." Daniel massaged the bridge of his nose. "Oh Lord, I don't know. Very well. Make me a promise."

Anything, Curtis almost said. "What do you want?"

"Promise me that you will not contact me, back in London, for, say, a fortnight. Promise me that you will think, and not with your prick either, about what you want. Promise me that you will not allow anything you have said or done this week to bind you in any way. Promise me, in fact, that if you decide that you're going to propose to Miss Merton—well, perhaps not her, but some delightful young lady—and pretend none of this ever happened, or even that on the whole you'd rather bugger a good honest English chap of your own class, you will simply go ahead and do it without a second's thought for my opinion."

"Daniel—"

Daniel rolled on his side, looking at Curtis with wide, dark eyes. "Promise me. And then, if you still want—anything, after you've had time to think about it, we'll talk, and if you decide you'd rather not, we'll part friends. Do you see?"

"What you mean is, I'm to do as I wish without giving a damn for you."

"If you give a damn for me, you'll do as I ask," retorted Daniel. "I can bear a great deal but I can't bear being an obligation."

"Or caves."

"Or, as you say, caves. I'm serious."

Curtis thought about it. He could feel Daniel's tension, a physical thing against him.

He had no idea what he wanted from Daniel, except that he should be there somehow. He only knew that his life outside the army had seemed purposeless, futureless, withered on the branch, and now, though he still had no idea what the future held, it was no longer empty. He had fought and made love this week, taken life and saved it, and it was all down to the man next to him.

Of course Daniel was right about the difference between their social circles. But he had spent the last year and a half drifting between clubs and sporting events and house parties, and it had been the driest, most pointless time of his life. Society was all very well; Curtis wanted companionship. More: he wanted Daniel, with his smooth skin and smoother tongue; wanted to get inside his fierce, brittle defences and protect the vulnerability within; wanted their growing bond so much that he flinched at the thought of its loss.

Curtis had no idea how this could possibly work, in London or anywhere else, but that was no reason to stop. Plans were for generals. He would approach this as he did everything, head on, forging forward step by step.

He looked down at Daniel, who was contemplating his chest hair like a man absorbed. "All right. I understand. You've scruples." Fears too, but he would no more have pointed that out than poked a mamba with a stick. "I'll make you that promise—a fortnight's consideration, no obligations, all you ask—if you'll tell me something in return now."

"What?" Daniel sounded wary.

"Subject to your stipulations and so forth..." Curtis leaned in and kissed him gently. "May I call on you?"

"Fuckin'*ell*, Curtis!" That came out as the purest East End. Curtis couldn't help grinning. Daniel narrowed his eyes and retrieved his poise along with his accent. "If you intend to start sending me posies with 'Wear this for my sake' cards, I shall *assault* you."

That wasn't an answer, except, in its defensive flare, it rather was. Curtis kissed him again, a little more demanding this time. "You've talked about what I want. I need to know what you want. May I call on you?"

"Yes, all *right*. If you must."

Curtis took hold of a handful of black hair and gave it a tug. "Does that mean you want me to?"

Daniel glowered. "Go to the devil, you overbearing, oversized sod."

Curtis lay back, satisfied, pulling him closer. He felt a whisper of a kiss against his chest.

"Get some sleep." Daniel yawned indicatively. "It's damned late. When will you go back in the morning?"

"I won't." Doubtless he should, it was what he'd intended, but Daniel had to be protected, and a fellow couldn't be expected to do everything. "The cavalry will be here soon enough. I'm staying with you."

Daniel's lips curved. He rubbed his head against Curtis's chest, catlike. "Now, quite seriously, my dear, get some rest."

Curtis wasn't reluctant; it had to be past three o'clock by his reckoning and he felt somewhat drained by the day. He wrapped his arm over Daniel's shoulders, steadied his mind, and slept.

Chapter Fourteen

"Wake up. Wake *up.*"

Curtis blinked into consciousness. The light was the yellow-grey of autumn dawn, which meant it must be past seven o'clock. His back was a solid line of soreness from lying on the hard floor, his mouth tasted furry and dry, the clothes he'd slept in were sweaty-cold, and Daniel was shaking his shoulder urgently.

"Wake up, you lump."

"What?"

"We're besieged."

Curtis was on his feet in a second, so fast his head swam slightly, crouching so as not to present a target to the window.

Daniel was kneeling by him, eyes wide in the dim light. "There's people moving out there. I saw March. I heard James Armstrong."

Curtis grabbed his Webley, checking it with the speed of long practice, and thrust handfuls of cartridges into his pockets. "Pat left a revolver. Can you shoot?"

"No."

Damn. "Then stay away from the windows. Is the door barred?"

"Yes."

At least he knew when to be brief. Curtis gave him a nod of acknowledgement as he pulled on his boots.

The mezzanine floor covered perhaps half of the interior, with a walkway running round the entire interior circumference of the absurd tower except where the stairs broke into it, allowing visitors to look out all around. Curtis, keeping low, manoeuvred himself to the front of the building. Daniel slithered round to the other side of the walkway, so he was a few feet away.

"Curtis!" It was a shout from outside. He recognised the voice and shot a look back at Daniel, who grimaced. "Curtis!"

He made a long arm, unlatched the closest window and pushed it open. "Sir Hubert," he called. "Good morning."

"Come out of there at once," shouted his host testily. "I don't know what you're playing at."

"No?" Curtis positioned himself to squat on his heels, back to the wall. "I dare say you'll find out if you wait long enough."

"Why don't you come down and discuss this like a sensible man?"

There was a soft rattle from the ground, someone trying the door.

"I think I can have a sensible conversation from here," Curtis said. "What would you like to talk about?"

"Where's Holt?" That was James Armstrong interrupting, sounding wild. "What have you done with Holt?"

Curtis glanced at Daniel, who shook his head.

"I've no idea where Holt is. Why would I?"

"You know where he is! You've got that bloody sneaking Yid in there, you filthy bugger!"

Curtis didn't give a damn for James Armstrong, except that he had every intention of beating him to a pulp before this was done. Still, the words were a drenching shock. He looked at Daniel again, and saw him mouth a sardonic, "Oooh," that steadied him as nothing else could have done.

"If you mean da Silva, yes, he's here. So?"

"So I'll kill him if you don't tell me where Holt is!"

Curtis grinned mirthlessly. "You'll have to get him first, you fucking shithouse cricket."

"Mind your language!" Sir Hubert sounded outraged.

Daniel craned his neck to glance out the window. "Oh, what the—Lady Armstrong's down there."

"Christ, really? Who else?"

"March. The other servant, Preston. They've all got those big guns, except her."

"Look out the other side," Curtis directed in a low voice.

Sir Hubert was calling up again. "There's no point in this. There's no way for this to end except in your disgrace."

"I think you're wrong." Curtis raised his brows at Daniel, who had been peering out of the windows. He shook his head, indicating no other arrivals.

Sir Hubert, James, March and Preston. Four guns to his one. But the folly was stone, the door thick new oak, the bar strong, his vantage point commanding. They could hold out here till the reinforcements arrived.

Sir Hubert made a pitying sort of noise. "I suppose you're thinking about the Foreign Office men you summoned."

"I expect he thinks they're coming to help him." Lady Armstrong's voice rippled with laughter.

"Help us, more like," James put in with a heavy sneer.

Curtis glanced over and saw Daniel's grim expression. The dark man's jaw was set.

"What are you talking about?" Curtis called out.

"Sir Maurice Vaizey's men," Sir Hubert said. "The ones you called when you telephoned your uncle with your tissue of lies. They'll be here by nine, I'm told."

Daniel muttered an obscenity. "They've a man on the inside, in the Bureau. Someone warned them."

"Hell," said Curtis quietly, then raised his voice. "Good. I'm looking forward to their arrival."

"I doubt that." Sir Hubert's voice was gloating. "You see, by the time they're here, there will be nothing for them to find. No documents, no photographs, no cameras. No evidence."

"Well, there is *one* set of photographs left," Lady Armstrong added, sugar sweet.

Sir Hubert laughed triumphantly. Curtis felt sweat spring in anticipation at the sound. "Quite right, my love. One set of photographs that will send the pair of you to gaol. Two years' hard labour for gross indecency. Let me see. We've made a set for Vaizey, of course, so he can see what his agent and his nephew get up to, and another for Henry. Poor chap, he *will* be disappointed in you. Another set for the police. A fourth for the papers, in case you think your money can keep this quiet. And a last set for us. Let's call it insurance. All of them sent to—a certain address, with instructions to forward them on unless I order otherwise by this afternoon."

"You'll be ruined," James said, voice thick with vindictive triumph.

Curtis shut his eyes. He didn't want to look at Daniel. He didn't want to look at anyone, ever again.

Sir Hubert was still talking. "Everything else has been burned by now. The cameras have been dismantled. There's no proof to be found at all."

"That's not quite right, is it?" Daniel called. "How exactly will you explain your possession of those photographs? If you use them, you prove our case."

"And there's my word and da Silva's," Curtis managed. His voice was treacherously hoarse. "How much investigation do you think you'll bear?"

"There won't be an investigation." Sir Hubert spoke with certainty. "Because you're going to deny everything. You'll tell Vaizey that it's all lies, a foolish game, some grudge of da Silva's. Whatever you have to in order to clear my name. Because if anyone should look into my affairs—well, the first thing they'll see is your affair. If you attack me, I'll ruin you. Do you understand?"

Curtis understood very well. His shoulders were heaving with the effort to breathe.

"I don't give a damn," he managed. "Go to the devil, you swine. I'll tell them everything and watch you swing from the gaolyard if I have to."

"For what?" Sir Hubert laughed, a fat, rich sort of noise that made Curtis's fists clench. "Jacobsdal? You can't prove a thing, any more than Lafayette could."

"Holt admitted it. He admitted it all."

"And will he admit that in front of a court?"

"He's in no position to," Daniel called out.

Curtis looked at him in shock. James Armstrong swore. "Where is he?" he roared. "What did you do with him?"

"He's with those men of Lafayette's. Where else?"

James bellowed an oath, and then Daniel and Curtis both hit the floor, covering their faces, as a window between them exploded in a shower of glass. The echoes of the shot rang in Curtis's ears, along with Sir Hubert's furious rebuke.

"Tetchy," called Daniel.

"What are you doing?" Curtis hissed. Daniel waved a hand, urging silence.

"You killed Holt," Sir Hubert said. "Was that you, Curtis? A fellow Blue?"

"A prick," said Daniel.

"He made you scream, you bloody dago," James roared.

Daniel grinned like a fox. "Pricks often do."

This time it was a fusillade, as James emptied his repeating rifle into the windows of the folly, yelling inarticulate rage. Curtis, flat on the floor, wrapped his arms over his head and screwed up his eyes to keep flying glass from his face, hoping Daniel was doing the same.

The echoes of gunfire died away, along with the tinkle of broken glass from shattered windows. Once the ringing in Curtis's ears had subsided, he could hear a low-voiced, angry exchange outside.

"What are you doing?" he demanded of Daniel, who was uncurling from a defensive ball on the floor. "What now? We can't let them get away with this. What the hell do we *do*?"

"How good a shot are you?" demanded Daniel, nodding at his hand.

"Good."

"Glad to hear it."

"What—?"

Daniel sat up, back to the wall, and shouted, "Hoi!" The voices outside fell silent.

"What d'you want?" called Sir Hubert.

"A sensible conversation. This interlude has been delightful and we've all enjoyed it, but we have some two hours at most before my colleagues arrive in force, and maybe less." That caused a murmur. Sir Hubert began to respond and Daniel interrupted impatiently, "I'm not bluffing, you fat fool. I've nothing to bluff with. I don't want to go to prison. I don't want Curtis to go to prison. So we need to establish— Oh, the devil with this. I'm coming out."

"What?" said almost everyone present.

"*I* am coming *out*, of the *door*, in about thirty seconds. Use that time to reflect on what will happen if Vaizey arrives to discover my bullet-riddled corpse. If you kill me, you will swing for murder, no matter what else you have or haven't done. Got it?"

"Holt—" James began angrily.

"Holt's dead. You aren't. If we speak like sensible men, we may all come out of this with whole skins."

"*Daniel*," hissed Curtis as the other man began to pick his way over the shattered glass to the stairs. "What are you doing?"

Daniel paused and looked round at him. "I need you to trust me. In the name of—last night, my dear Viking. If you could dissuade anyone who tries to kill me, that would be marvellous too. But, Archie, I beg you, trust me now. And if this doesn't work—" He gave a quick, twisted smile, and Curtis saw the fear that it concealed. "It's been a pleasure."

"No. Stop." Curtis reached out, but there was no way he could scramble forward over the broken glass fast enough to reach him. Daniel shook his head and hurried down the stairs. "Daniel!"

"Get to the window," snapped Daniel from below.

"Shit!" Curtis swung back to the window, taking up a stance that let him see the action on the ground. His Webley was no substitute for a sniper's rifle, but the enemy on the ground was close enough that he felt confident he could drop whoever he aimed at.

Daniel was going a lot closer to them than that.

He felt a strange, fatalistic calm close over him as he heard Daniel lift the bar. The group below were frozen, staring. James Armstrong had appropriated Preston's shotgun, discarding his own emptied rifle. He and March had their guns trained on the doorway as Daniel emerged. Sir Hubert held his rifle over his arm, like a gentleman out for a morning stroll picking off pheasants.

Three, Curtis thought. He could shoot three.

Daniel stepped forward, into Curtis's range of vision. James moved forward, red-faced and buoyed by rage, swinging the butt of his gun violently. Daniel jumped back, and Curtis put a bullet into the earth by James's foot.

"Christ!" yelled James, leaping away.

"More where that came from," Curtis called down.

"Quite," said Daniel. "Curtis is a damned good shot, and an angry man. Don't provoke him. And don't forget, if you shoot me, you will swing for murder. Vaizey doesn't tolerate dead agents."

Sir Hubert was looking at him without liking. "Well? What do you want?"

"Cards on the table," said Daniel. "You've destroyed the evidence, you have photographs that will ruin Curtis. But if you use them, you prove our case. I call that a stalemate. Neither of us can accuse the other without accusing ourselves. Right?"

Sir Hubert gave a stiff nod.

"But it's a little late for that," Daniel went on. "Vaizey is coming up here expecting to find evidence of blackmail. He's not going to believe that Curtis was playing some schoolboy joke."

"That's your problem," James put in angrily.

"Quite," snapped Sir Hubert.

"So tell me what you want." Daniel was speaking to Sir Hubert only, ignoring the rest. "I'm in Vaizey's confidence. I can make this plausible. I know what the Bureau knows, I can pin it all on a scapegoat, and you'll get away scot-free. With everything. Vaizey has no idea about Lafayette or Jacobsdal yet. We can keep that quiet, if we work together."

Curtis could feel the sweat cold on his back. His left hand held the Webley rock steady, but he could feel the tremor building in his right, a slow swell of rage.

Archie, trust me now.

"You'll betray your office, will you?" Sir Hubert demanded.

"Of course he will," said James. "It's just as Holt said. You can't trust his sort."

"To hell with my office." Daniel's voice was low and vicious. "I don't give a damn for Jacobsdal, or King, or country. Why would I? This country doesn't give a damn for me. I do this job for money, that's all. I don't want to go to prison, nor do you. I can make sure we all get out of this. But we have to do this together."

"What about Curtis?"

Daniel laughed, an unpleasant sound. "Lovely bloke, hung like a prize bull, but *not* a bright man. I can lead him around by his cock, don't worry."

James squawked with fury, sounding like he was being throttled by his own outrage. Daniel laughed again and put on an exaggerated version of his drawing-room manner. "Forgive my vulgarity. I thought we weren't playing games any more. Curtis will do as he's told."

Curtis breathed evenly, in and out. His right hand was shaking. He could move the Webley's muzzle just a fraction, aim it at Daniel's skull. Pull the trigger.

Trust me, trust me, trust me...

"Then do it. What else do you need to know?" Sir Hubert asked.

"How you want to play this. Who's being thrown to the wolf. Let's make an arrangement." Daniel jerked his head in the direction of James and Lady Armstrong. "Do you want them hamstrung, cut off or dead?"

Sir Hubert was gobbling like a turkey. "What the— Are you mad?"

"No?" said Daniel, surprised. "You don't want rid of them? I'd assumed you'd kill two birds with one stone."

"Why the devil would I *want rid of* my wife and son?" Sir Hubert was an odd shade of puce.

"Well, they're cuckolding you."

The words, said with casual certainty, dropped like stones on ice. Sir Hubert stood quite still. Curtis felt a fierce, prideful smile curving his lips.

"You beautiful bastard," he murmured, and held the Webley ready.

"Tripe," James said. "How dare you. Pater, don't listen to this rubbish."

Lady Armstrong was giving angry little gasps. "Hubert, I hope you don't intend to let this man speak of me like that."

"You're a damned liar," Sir Hubert told Daniel, raising the shotgun. Curtis moved the Webley, aiming at his host's sweaty forehead.

"If you shoot me, you'll hang," Daniel reminded him.

"You're lying. Admit it!"

"All right, all right, I'm lying." There was a contemptuous sneer in Daniel's voice. "Of course your wife doesn't prefer a lusty young lad between her legs to a fat old man sweating away. Of course James would never let you down, when has he ever done that? Of course the servants don't know."

Sir Hubert's head jolted, as if struck. Preston was staring straight ahead.

"March?" said Sir Hubert. "Is this—"

"Darling, of course it's not true," said Lady Armstrong. "Honestly, you must see what he's doing."

"March?"

March glanced at his master and away. He opened his mouth and shut it, uncertain for once. "Sir..."

"It's not his fault," Daniel said. "After all, you already knew, really, didn't you? All those energetic walks you don't go on. All those trips to London while you work, those jaunts to the caves together—"

James was purple-faced. "Shut up you bloody dago. Shut up!"

"If you like." Daniel grinned. "For the record, though, Armstrong...your mother's a whore."

"Don't you talk about her!" James screamed, and there was all the betrayal anyone needed in that protective flare.

"You little swine." Sir Hubert was staring at his son.

"Pater—" James said urgently.

"Ungrateful worthless beast." The old man's voice was thick.

"Yes," Daniel said. "If only he'd died instead of Martin. Haven't you always thought so?"

Sir Hubert's face said everything. Father and son stared at each other, mouths working, neither able to find words.

"Hubert, listen to me," said Lady Armstrong urgently. "This is all lies."

"Holt told us everything," Daniel said. "He begged for his life. Gave us all the juicy details." He looked at James. "You might have chosen someone more trustworthy to brag to."

Lady Armstrong swung to glare at James, lips drawn back over her pretty white teeth in a snarl. Sir Hubert gave a painful gasp. And James Armstrong howled his rage and frustration as he brought his shotgun up in a fluent motion, with Daniel at point-blank range.

Curtis shot him through the temple.

James's head snapped back with a spray of blood. His body toppled and fell. There was a second's silence, then both Lady Armstrong and Sir Hubert screamed, "No!"

Lady Armstrong fell to her knees, reaching for the corpse whose blue eyes gazed sightlessly up. "Jimmy," she sobbed. "Jimmy, darling? Jimmy!"

Sir Hubert stared, jaw slack, gun loose in his grip. Preston was backing away. March had his shotgun pointed at Daniel, but he didn't look about to shoot. He stared from master to mistress.

"James," rasped Sir Hubert. He took a step forward, almost tottering. "Sophie."

"Don't come near us." Lady Armstrong leaned over the body like a bitch protecting her pups, face distorted, tears running down her cheeks. Her voice was raw. "Get away, you stupid hateful fat filthy old pig. Get away from me!"

"I expect Vaizey will be able to arrange some sort of pardon if one of you talks," Daniel said. "The other will swing, of course. Who will it be?"

Sophie Armstrong turned to him, face distorted with grief, and began to speak. A single shot cracked, and blood bloomed across her chest. She stared stupidly up, mouth open, and then fell forward.

"Oh, sir," said March.

Sir Hubert lowered his gun, gazing at the body of his wife slumped over the body of his son. At the window Curtis had the Webley in a two-handed grip, gaze locked on the old man. He was trying to say something, eyes vague, mouth working. He raised the rifle. The barrel wavered. Then, in an abrupt motion, he reversed it, jammed the end of the barrel awkwardly into his mouth, and reached for the trigger. His arm was just long enough.

Curtis winced at the shot. He looked away from the bloody ruin of Sir Hubert's skull, out of the window, and saw something on the hills.

"Hell and damnation!" He took one swift look to check March wasn't about to fire, then hurtled down the stairs, leaping over breaking glass and taking the steps in three strides. He slowed as he came out of the folly door, so as not to startle March into shooting, but the servant was bent over his master's body, murmuring. Preston was nowhere to be seen.

"Where's the other one?" he demanded, scanning the trees around.

"Gone," said Daniel. "He's unarmed, and has as much to lose as anyone."

Curtis looked him over. Dishevelled in the baggy stolen clothes, grubby and unwashed, heavy black stubble already turning to beard, face grey in the thin morning light.

"Daniel," he said quietly.

March straightened to stare at them. Curtis levelled the Webley at him. "Gun down. Don't be a fool, man, your master's dead."

March's face worked, but he lowered his shotgun.

"Step away. Daniel, take it. Sir Maurice is coming, I saw at least four motorcars. We don't have long."

"They'll get you," March said venomously as Daniel took the gun from his hand with extreme caution. "You'll be found out. Sodomite."

Curtis punched him, without warning, in the sweet spot under the chin, and watched him drop. He shrugged at Daniel's look. "I don't want him in the way. Come on."

As they hurried through the young woods that Sir Hubert would never see grow, Curtis said, "How did you know?"

"It was glaringly obvious. You didn't notice?"

"You made that happen on *guesswork*?"

"No," said Daniel. "Yes. I did. I— Hell." He spun away, doubling over, and retched, coughing and choking as he spat out thin watery vomit. "Shit. Oh shit."

Curtis grabbed him, hands on slender shoulders as they heaved. "It's all right. Shh. You're safe."

"They're not." Daniel wiped his mouth with the back of a shaking hand and straightened cautiously. "The devil. I call myself a pacifist. That was wholesale slaughter."

"You didn't do it."

"I made it happen. All of it. Even James, you wouldn't have had to do that if—"

"I would. I promised myself the blighter some time ago."

Daniel looked up at that. "Yes, you did, didn't you? The soldier at work. I wish I had your singleness of purpose."

"Those swine murdered my men at Jacobsdal. They all knew about the sabotage, the bodies in the sinkhole. The three of them can go straight to hell. And we have to get to the house."

"Right," said Daniel, and then, "I'm sorry, but you do realise we've lost."

"We can try."

"We can't. You heard Armstrong. The photographs are already on their way to wherever it may be, we don't know because I killed them. I've ruined you. I'm sorry. It seemed like a good idea at the time."

Curtis grabbed him, pulling him close. Daniel dropped his head, not meeting his eyes.

"Look at me. It's not your fault. Christ, man, you've done what you could."

"To destroy your life."

"No." Curtis wrapped his arms round him, not caring if anyone might be there to see. It hardly mattered now. "There was nothing there to destroy."

"Say that again from a gaol cell," Daniel muttered into his chest.

"It won't come to that. We may have to leave the country in a hurry, that's all."

Daniel looked up, his face drawn with pain, eyes glistening bright. "It's not all. Your family. Your position."

Curtis kissed him, gently but firmly. "You faced all that. So can I. No guilt, it doesn't suit you."

"It ought to." Daniel pulled away and hurried on towards the house. "I have made such a damned mess of this. Vaizey's going to murder me, and so he should."

"Nonsense."

"I've lost the evidence of who's betraying their country, provided a trio of corpses to be explained away, and ruined his nephew. He's going to murder me."

Put like that, it did seem likely. "Come on," Curtis said as they crunched up the gravel in front of the house, in step. "Let's face this."

Chapter Fifteen

The front door stood open. In the otherwise empty hallway, Lambdon lay unconscious on the floor with blood trickling sluggishly from a nasty wound in his scalp.

"What the—"

"Ssh." Curtis frowned, looking around, then took a few long strides to the library door.

"Let me," he mouthed, lifting his revolver and indicating the other man should stay behind him.

Daniel stepped back. Curtis took a breath, elbowed the door open, swung into the room and stopped dead, with the muzzle of a Holland and Holland shotgun pointing directly in his face.

"Oh, it's you," said Patricia Merton, lowering the gun. "You've been a while, I must say."

Curtis stared at her. Then he stared at the other two occupants of the room: the servant Wesley, kneeling, face to the wall and hands behind back; and Fenella Carruth, holding a pretty little Colt ladies' revolver with obvious competence. He gaped at her. She gave him a sparkling smile.

Beside him, Daniel made a strangled noise, and pointed at the open storeroom door. Curtis could see papers and photographs spilled on the floor.

"Are you after that business?" asked Pat, jerking her head. "It's all perfectly safe, if that's what you were wondering."

Daniel bolted into the storeroom. Curtis managed, "How?"

"Well, we heard them," Pat said.

"Plotting," put in Fen with relish.

"Lots of tramping around this morning and a great deal of subdued shouting. It sounded very like something had gone wrong, so when the Armstrongs left, we thought we might take a look. And there were this precious fellow and the atrocious Mr. Lambdon lighting the fire and taking out piles of papers and photographs, which I realised must be all that nastiness you told me about. And I thought, well, I doubt Archie wants *that* destroyed before your friends arrive. So we asked them to stop."

"We asked very nicely," said Fen, tipping her gun.

"Did they burn anything at all?" Daniel called from the storeroom.

"No, they'd only just started to set the fire. It's all there. Well, almost. Fen, dear?"

Fen turned away and tugged something out of her bodice. She came over and handed an envelope to Curtis.

"You should have these," she said. "We'd have burned them if they'd got the fire lit."

Curtis pulled out the contents and glanced down at the top photograph—himself, Daniel; he flinched away from the explicitness of it. He turned the sheaf over hastily, not knowing what to say to Fen.

She gazed up at him, serious for a second, and then quite suddenly stood on tiptoes to kiss his cheek.

"You don't need to worry about us, Archie. I know it's harder for you, of course, but—well, it's surprising what one can get away with, in society, you know. People notice far less than one might fear. We've found it so, haven't we, Pat?"

Pat rolled her eyes and gave Fen a look of fond exasperation. Curtis looked from one woman to the other. Realisation dawned.

Fen twinkled roguishly and leaned in to whisper, "And I do admire your taste. I've always said, Mr. da Silva is *terribly* handsome."

"Fenella Carruth!" said Pat. "Leave that poor man alone."

"Archie, are you holding what I think you are?" demanded Daniel from the storeroom door.

"Thank the ladies." Curtis gave a helpless shrug.

Daniel looked at him for a second, then fell dramatically to his knees, arms wide. "Miss Merton, Miss Carruth. Both or either. Marry me."

"What an appalling offer," said Pat, as Fen went off into peals of laughter. "And get up, you absurd creature, that's motorcars I hear on the drive."

Curtis fastened his suitcase. He had packed it himself; the house was in chaos, and in any case, he did not want any servants to see his bloodstained clothes, let alone those dreadful photographs. They were safely stowed at the bottom of his Gladstone bag, ready to be burned when he had a chance. He didn't intend to lose sight of the bag till then.

He had propped a painting over the mirror and the hole in the wall. He wondered if he would ever trust a mirror again.

Eight of Vaizey's men had arrived, all armed, along with his formidable uncle, and had swept Daniel up in a burst of activity from which everyone else was firmly excluded. The bodies of the Armstrongs had been retrieved, along with March. He and Wesley were maintaining a sullen silence, and had not tried mounting counter-accusations against Curtis and Daniel. They both fell back on doing what the master said and knowing nowt.

The Graylings had departed in a shocked and bewildered hurry. Lambdon would require medical attention for a fractured skull. It seemed that Fen had passed his wife a couple of telling pictures, whereupon the drab Mrs. Lambdon had brained her husband with a table lamp.

There was a quiet knock on the door. Curtis hadn't heard anyone come along the passage, and his heart leapt at the realisation.

"Come in."

Silent as ever, Daniel slipped in and closed the door. He had washed, shaved and changed, Curtis realised. He looked presentable, and exhausted, and beautiful.

"You found your case, then?"

"Yes, they had my things in the service corridor. Thank goodness. An entire new wardrobe would be an unwelcome expense." Daniel gave him a glancing look that slipped away almost at once.

"Daniel..."

"You should be safe." Daniel spoke hurriedly. "Any accusations will seem obvious spite, but in any case I don't think anyone's going to admit they know anything more than they have to. The responsibility is going on the dead, where it belongs. Keep your head and you'll keep everything." He hesitated a fraction. "I'm glad. You've your life back."

"If I do, it's thanks to you. You saved me, Daniel."

"I'm quite sure that was the other way around."

"Then we saved each other. Do you have time now?"

"Ten minutes, if that." Daniel gave a little, miserable smile. "Long enough to say goodbye."

Curtis brushed a thumb gently over his lips, and frowned as Daniel turned his face away. "I don't want to say goodbye."

"You will. Back in London, in your world. You know it's true. I'd rather part friends now than have you embarrassed to be seen with me, or looking for ways to tell me it's done with. I'd rather end it now. While I can."

"What? No. You promised. You had my promise—two weeks and all that—and I've yours. I'm damned if I'll let you go back on that."

Daniel sagged against the wall. "I wish you'd listen. This is not going to work."

"That's what you said this morning about the photographs."

"Yes, and how many miracles do you think we're entitled to?"

"What are you frightened of?" Curtis demanded.

"Frightened?" Daniel's mouth twisted. "I'm frightened that I'll hurt you, you idiot. That you'll be hurt through me. You've no idea what it is to be sneered at for what you are. To have people cut you dead, or look at you with contempt, or have your friends and family turn their backs— You don't know what that's like. I don't *want* you to know what that's like. God damn it, I saw your face when you thought your uncles would get those bloody photographs!"

"Daniel—"

"No. I can't do that to you. To see you look like that, because of me—I couldn't bear it."

Curtis reached out and cupped Daniel's face, feeling the freshly shaven skin smooth against his palm. "Enough about me. What are *you* frightened of?"

Daniel shut his eyes. He said, very quietly, "I don't want to be hurt either. And I don't think I've ever met anyone who could hurt me as much as you."

"I don't intend to hurt you."

"I know you don't." He took a deep breath. "I think you will."

"No. Daniel—"

"It's very easy to be swept away when you're getting your cock sucked." That nasty bite was back in Daniel's voice. "But I assure you the appeal will diminish when the whispers start."

Curtis's fingers bit into Daniel's chin, forcing it up. "Look at me. I am not that bastard at Cambridge. I'm ten years older—"

"And have about five years less experience than he did then."

"Experience of this, perhaps. I've plenty of experience facing things a damn sight more dangerous than a gross indecency charge."

"Danger." Daniel's voice was scathing. "You're rich, your uncle's Sir Maurice Vaizey, you'd have to bugger the Chancellor of the Exchequer on the Woolsack to get yourself gaoled. We both know you could get out of that sort of trouble. It's the gossip and the giggles, the cold shoulders and the awful talks with your uncles, and the *looks*— God damn it, you can't even begin to understand, can you? If you had the imagination to feel what you're blithely letting yourself in for, you'd be thanking me for saving you from it before we both get hurt."

"Well, I don't, so I'm not. I told you before, I'm not hiding behind you. I've a say in this."

"Yes, and so do I, and I'm telling you now, it's done with." Daniel's face was very pale. "You may not call on me, and I don't want to see you, and I am not going to be instrumental in your ruin, and you will not blame me for it. That's an end to it. Don't look at me like that."

"I had your promise," Curtis said. An awful, hollow sense was growing in his chest that Daniel meant it, that he would not be persuaded. "You gave me your word—"

"That's dagos for you," Daniel bit out. "Can't trust them."

"Archie!" The voice came from the corridor, a stentorian bellow. Sir Maurice, his uncle.

"Hell's teeth. Daniel—"

Daniel was already moving away, staring out of the window.

"Archie!"

"Here, sir," Curtis managed to call.

Sir Maurice Vaizey slammed into the room, glancing from his man to his nephew, thick brows set in their habitual scowl. "Da Silva? I thought you were resting. What the devil are you lolling about in here for?"

"I am quite rejuvenated." Daniel arched a brow at his chief. "Your charming nephew and I have been having a *delightful* tête-à-tête."

Incredibly, he had adopted his most effete, drawling manner. Curtis glanced at his uncle with apprehension, waiting for the explosion, but Sir Maurice appeared unmoved.

"Stop playing the fool. What are you up to?"

"Discussing the coroner's inquest, dear sir. I felt we should get our stories straight on poor James."

"You won't be giving evidence," Sir Maurice told him. "Any self-respecting jury would hang you on sight and I shouldn't blame them. Go on, get out, make yourself useful, if you're capable of it. I need to speak to Archie."

"Charmed as ever. Sir. Curtis." Daniel left, without a backward glance, and with a pronounced sway in his hips.

"Bloody pansy," Sir Maurice said, with an astonishing lack of heat. "You'd hardly believe he was one of my better men. Well, I wouldn't, after the mess he's made of this."

"That was my fault, sir," Curtis said. "I got in his way."

"Yes, you did. Why didn't you tell me what you were planning, boy, before heading up here like a lone crusader?"

"Lafayette said he'd already been to see you, sir. He said you didn't believe him."

"He did, and I didn't." Sir Maurice snorted. "More fool me. Well, we've three corpses—or four; is Mr. Holt's body likely to turn up?"

Curtis shut his suitcase. "No, sir."

"Good. Three corpses and a cabinet full of treachery, sodomy and adultery. I'm going to need your silence on this, Archie."

"Good God, sir, as if you need to ask."

Sir Maurice nodded. "You'll have to stay up for the coroner's inquest on James Armstrong, we can't have you committed for trial. I'm going to get da Silva out of the way, and we'll give you a story that doesn't feature him."

"He'd be perfectly capable of making a good impression on a jury," Curtis said. "You must know he puts that manner on."

His uncle gave him a look that blended a moderate amount of affection with a great deal of irritation. "You don't need to be chivalrous, my boy, he's not actually a woman. I need him out of this because I have a damned sight more work for him to do, and I don't want his name bruited about too widely in association with this business."

"Work? Good Lord, sir, he was almost killed not two days ago—"

"That's his job. Yours, at the moment, is to tell me everything you know. Now, pay attention."

Sir Maurice's debriefing was thorough to the point of madness; his instructions on dealing with the inevitable inquest so detailed that Curtis was tempted to plead guilty and ask for gaol. He was closeted with his uncle for four hours, and when he finally emerged, it was to learn that Daniel had left for London. There was no message.

Chapter Sixteen

It was eleven days before he returned to London.

The inquest had been relatively plain sailing. He, Miss Carruth and Miss Merton all testified that James Armstrong had been drinking too much and distressed about his friend's departure. Curtis's account, uncontested, told how a drunken James Armstrong had sprayed the empty folly with bullets, then shot his stepmother, how he had shot James, just too late to prevent murder, and how Sir Hubert had turned the gun on himself. March did not appear in his account, or at the inquest.

The Graylings were in attendance, tight-lipped and miserable, but were not called. The Lambdons did not appear. Mr. Lambdon had not recovered from his head injury, it was said; his wife was receiving care in a sanatorium.

Daniel da Silva was mentioned in passing as a guest who had left the house long before the terrible events. James's mental collapse was linked to his friend Mr. Holt's abrupt departure, but to the coroner's annoyance, Mr. Holt could not be found. He had testy words to say about that.

There was a brief difficulty over why Curtis had gone out for a morning stroll with a loaded revolver, but Vaizey had briefed him well. He held up his right hand and explained that he was trying to accustom himself to his disability; and if anyone felt that a one-handed man using wildlife for target practice seemed dangerously eccentric, that was outweighed by natural respect for a wounded war hero, which the coroner expressed throughout in glowing terms. The whole thing was thoroughly embarrassing.

Worse came after. Vaizey had left him in the company of an agent named Cannon, who explained that he couldn't return to London till the nine days' wonder over a rich man's familial murder and suicide had died down, and who then proceeded to interrogate him for every scrap of information he could recall, on Holt, on the Armstrongs, on Lambdon, over and over. Cannon informed him, sourly, that he'd had his eye on Holt for some time; the man's untimely death had lost their best chance at discovering the extent of the blackmail network and the channels through which information was flowing to the Continent. He went so far as to suggest that England would have been better served with Holt alive and Daniel dead, at which point Curtis had stopped cooperating and started expressing his desire to go home in forceful terms.

Eleven days. If Daniel had kept his promise, Curtis would have been counting them off, waiting to see his lover.

He had thought of it all, endlessly, over long walks and angry, solitary nights. He had thought about the possibility of social disgrace, about disappointing his uncles, about what he would do with the rest of his life. He had thought of Daniel, who didn't back down for Sir Maurice Vaizey, walking away from him.

Now he was back in London, at last, in a small, stuffy room in a nondescript building somewhere off Whitehall, facing his uncle across a table.

"It seemed to go well," Sir Maurice said. "No repercussions so far. There's been some fluttering in the dovecotes here, but less than one might have expected. Have you heard about Armstrong's will?"

"Yes."

"That's rather a stroke of luck—"

"No."

Sir Maurice eyed him thoughtfully. "It's a fair sum, my boy, and you can hardly refuse it without raising questions that I'm afraid I don't want you to raise."

"I will not take his money."

Armstrong's will had left the majority of his estate to his son and wife, with the residue to be split between the dependents of the men who died at Jacobsdal and the wounded survivors. The idea of Armstrong writing that, believing that doling out a little cash would somehow absolve him, had put Curtis into a rage that had led to him splitting a knuckle on a wall.

Of course, it wasn't a little cash. Since son and wife had predeceased him, Sir Hubert's bequest was now the bulk of his fortune, whatever might be left when the debts were paid. It was filthy, tainted money, but if the other mutilated men, the widows and orphans, didn't know that, they could take it as some compensation for their losses. Curtis couldn't.

"Don't be too fastidious, my boy," Sir Maurice said. "You wouldn't want to put anyone else off claiming their share, now, would you?"

"I'm putting my share back in the pot for the others. Nobody will think twice, sir. I'm a wealthy man."

Sir Maurice sighed pointedly. Curtis was a wealthy man in large part because his uncle had managed his inheritance since he had been orphaned at the age of two months. "I take a proprietorial interest in your prosperity, Archie. And at such time as you decide to meet a nice young lady and settle down, you will thank me."

"I'm already thankful, sir. May I ask if you called me here to discuss this?"

"I didn't." Sir Maurice sat back and steepled his fingers. "I've a problem, and I wonder if you can help me."

"With pleasure, sir. What is it?"

"I wouldn't jump at it too quickly." Sir Maurice gave a sour smile. "I suppose you've worked out how the Armstrongs knew you and da Silva were holed up in that absurd building."

"Da Silva said someone in your office must have talked, sir. Someone telephoned Peakholme to give them everything I'd told you."

"Quite." Sir Maurice looked like he was chewing unripe gooseberries. "Someone sold da Silva to the enemy. I assumed the guilty party would become apparent. He hasn't."

"You don't know who talked?" Curtis repeated, incredulously.

"No."

"You do understand we could have been killed." Curtis had to fight to keep a rein on his patience at his uncle's calm tone. "If I wasn't a left-handed shot, and da Silva wasn't so quick-thinking—"

"I'm well aware of that. I don't know who it was."

"I think you need to find out before you send him on any further missions. Don't you?" Curtis realised that he had half-risen from his chair, and his uncle was regarding him with a quizzical expression. He sat back down, managing a smile. "I feel strongly on this, sir. I killed two men to save the fellow's life. I shouldn't like that to be in vain."

"Oddly enough, nor should I." Sir Maurice tapped his fingers together. "My problem with da Silva is twofold. He's got a damned nasty tongue, and he's a coward."

"He's nothing of the kind!" Curtis was almost shouting, and this time he really didn't care. "Good God, sir, how can you sit behind a desk and say that? He walked up to three men pointing guns in his face, unarmed—"

"Yes, unarmed," Sir Maurice repeated. "He won't learn to shoot, let alone carry a knife. I don't suppose he's ever raised a fist in anger. I grant you he's got plenty of nerve, but he's a physical coward. Most of his sort are, I believe."

Curtis didn't know if "his sort" meant Daniel's race, politics or preferences, and he didn't care. He held a deep affection for his uncle, but on this point, he could go to hell. "There's all sorts of courage, sir. And if you've a better man in your office, I should like to meet him."

Sir Maurice waved that away. "The point is, he can't look after himself. And I can't send anyone to look after him. Not just because there's someone in my department that I can't trust, either. I've tried to partner da Silva three times now, and nobody can stomach the blasted man." He gave Curtis a slanting look. "Apparently, you can."

"I've a thick skin, sir."

"And a kindly nature." Sir Maurice gave one of his rare genuine smiles. "You remind me of your mother sometimes. She had a soft heart for lame dogs too."

"I do not," said Curtis, revolted.

Sir Maurice leaned forward. "We both know you need something to do with yourself, Archie. I need someone I can trust. And da Silva needs someone at his back. I've work for him, and it may be dangerous. I dare say I shouldn't ask this, and you may refuse if you don't think you can tolerate the man any longer. But I'd like to offer you a job."

Curtis left the office a few hours later, with a piece of paper bearing Daniel's address.

It would be the height of stupidity to go round there directly, he told himself, as he caught the omnibus in the direction of Holborn. He should write first. Arrange a convenient time. Give the man a chance to refuse.

God knew he'd made himself clear back at Peakholme. This visit wouldn't be welcome. Curtis considered that as he hopped off the 'bus at the British Museum stop and ventured into the new buildings of shabby-genteel Bloomsbury. Daniel was fiercely proud, defensive to a fault. Curtis shouldn't force his company on him.

And what if he was entertaining other company? That was an unwelcome reflection, but it had to be faced. Why would Daniel not have a lover in London, or several?

He threaded his way through long streets of grey-bricked houses, dodging perambulators and flower sellers, wondering about that. He knew his own mind. No doubt there, after eleven endless, restless nights, clutching at every minute of those few precious hours in the folly, already afraid he'd begin to forget. But what Daniel really felt, what he wanted, whether he had pushed Curtis away purely for his sake or because he had no need for an inexperienced, overfond fool, whether he shared Curtis's sense of a connection between them that was more than physical and more than mental...

Curtis didn't know any of that and, he thought as he pulled the bell of the small boarding house, he was an utter idiot simply to charge forward. Any chap with sense would handle this with discretion, and consideration, and tact. Nobody in his right mind would just knock at the man's door.

The landlady showed him up to the first-floor landing and indicated the door. He knocked. There was a faint sound from inside that was almost certainly a curse, the door was pulled open with clear irritation, and Daniel was there.

He was in his shirtsleeves and waistcoat, cuffs rolled back. His hair was unoiled, and tumbled, as though someone had been grabbing at it. There was ink on his fingers and he was wearing wire-rimmed spectacles. Curtis was captivated by the spectacles.

Daniel blinked twice, then snatched the spectacles off his nose. "Curtis." He stepped back to let him in, and shut the landlady firmly out. "What the hell do you want?"

"I want to see you."

"I told you. No." Daniel put the reading glasses on his desk. It was a small deal table, piled with papers. The top sheets were covered in Daniel's looping scrawl: short lines with a lot of scratching out and insertions.

"Are you writing a poem?" Curtis asked, fascinated.

Daniel turned the sheet over in a pointed fashion. There was writing on the back as well. He hissed with annoyance and slapped a newspaper on top of the pile. "I don't care for observation."

"No." Curtis looked round the room. It was a humble sort of place, rather cramped and with faded furnishings. A small fire burned in the inadequate grate, and the coals were low in the scuttle.

"Can I help you?" enquired Daniel waspishly. He propped his shoulders against the wall, arms folded over his chest. "Since I told you that you were not welcome to visit..."

"This is a professional call."

"Really? Did I invade someone's country?"

"Your profession," Curtis clarified, and added, "Not the poetry."

"Yes, I grasped that, thank you. What about it?"

Daniel was clearly not in an accommodating mood. No point beating about the bush, then. "I thought I should let you know, we're going to be working together."

That broke through the facade. Daniel stared at him. "We what?"

"Working together. My uncle asked me to. In case you find yourself in a scrap."

Daniel's expression suggested a scrap was imminent. "I do not need a nursemaid," he said through gritted teeth. "I do not want a partner. I have never wanted a partner."

"No. My uncle told me you've already driven three chaps off with that vicious tongue of yours."

"Quite. Of course, if a man favours me with his opinion of bloody sodomites and bloody Jews, that is simply the civilised exchange of views. Whereas if I give him my opinion of his intellect and physical prowess in return, that's my vicious tongue."

"I like your tongue."

Daniel's brows shot up, and it was not a mannered movement. He recovered his poise. "How daring of you to say so."

"Not really." Curtis stepped forward, one stride closer. "I know you don't need a nursemaid. But my uncle has just given me a reason to be close to you. If you want me to be."

Daniel's dark eyes were unblinking. "A reason only your uncle will know. And meanwhile, the whispers start."

"He told me there was a chance people might speculate, if I was seen to form a friendship with you. I told him I didn't care. I don't." Daniel gave him a sceptical look. "I don't. He's given me a reason that he and Sir Henry will be happy with. If I needn't worry about my uncles, the rest of the world can go hang."

"So you say now."

"You don't hide," Curtis said. "You could convert, you could dress conservatively, you could speak like a—an officer, if you wanted. You don't *pretend* all the time. Why do you insist I should?"

"You've been pretending for thirty years," Daniel flashed.

"I'm sick of it. I was going to come here anyway, Sir Maurice just made it easy. Daniel, I want to be with you. And if I can't have that—" He stared into the dark eyes, willing him to understand. "I still shan't go back to the pretence. I've spent my life in this state of—of murkiness, as if I've been in one of your blasted fishponds all this time. Dark water. And I won't put my head back under."

Daniel's eyes widened, then he turned his face away. Voice biting and very brittle, he said, "No, poetry really *isn't* your field, is it. I suggest you leave the metaphors to me."

It hurt like a physical blow. Curtis stared at him, and suddenly realised that he was sick of talk, sick of trying to breach defences with weapons he was no damned good at using.

"You're right," he said. "I'm no poet. Let's do this the military way."

"What—" Daniel began, and then gave a strangled squawk as Curtis jerked him forward, pinioning Daniel's left arm to his waist and gripping his other wrist hard. He leaned in against him, using fifteen stone of solid muscle to press him to the wall.

Daniel glared up at him. "What the devil are you doing?"

"Shutting your damned mouth," said Curtis, and kissed him as forcefully as he could.

Daniel made a noise of outrage against his lips, struggling with what felt like genuine effort. It did him no good. Curtis was far stronger, and had restrained plenty of men, albeit not while kissing them, and he easily overrode Daniel's attempts to break free, forcing his mouth over lips that moved with what were probably curses. Daniel's writhing was bumping their hips together, and Curtis deliberately pressed closer, body to body.

Daniel twisted violently to get his mouth free, and managed, "...fucking Viking!"

"Black mamba."

"Black what?"

"A kind of snake. Dark, beautiful and appallingly foul-tempered."

"Sod you."

Daniel lunged at him. Their mouths met again, hard and hungry. Curtis didn't restrain his strength and felt Daniel's savage response, teeth digging into his lips. He could feel Daniel's arousal, pressing hard against his thigh, his movements now all about rubbing bodies rather than winning freedom, and though it was far outside his experience, Curtis knew an overwhelming urge to pick him up, throw him down on the bed, do things that would make him scream aloud and shatter his defences for good. He was bloody well going to find out what those things would be.

He drove his hips forward, pushing Daniel back against the wall, and relished the gasp against his mouth.

"Pax," Daniel managed, turning his head sideways for air. "Pax. All right, what did that prove? That you're bigger than me?"

"You want me. This isn't over." Curtis loosened his grip on Daniel's arms and leaned back, looking down at his bruised lips and dark, unfathomable eyes. There was a moment of silence and hard breathing.

"That," Daniel said at last, "was ungentlemanly."

"I'll be a gentleman if you will."

They stared at each other, chests rising and falling. A lock of Daniel's tousled hair was falling into his eyes. Curtis brushed it away, fingertips skimming the skin, felt rather than saw Daniel's tiny sway towards him.

He said, more gently, "I meant what I said. I'm glad this happened, between us."

"*Please.*" Daniel spat the word. "Don't pretend I've done you any favours."

"You have. You don't know how much. Look, Daniel, I want you. I've never wanted anyone like this before, and I don't suppose I will again. I want you to argue with me, and make me laugh, and laugh at me, or with me. I want the appalling things you say and the modern nonsense you spout. But if you honestly don't want to carry on as we were, then I'll accept that. I'll have to. All I ask is that if you send me away, it's for your sake, not mine. I don't need a nursemaid either."

There was utter silence for a moment.

Daniel pushed the heels of his trembling hands over his eyes. "I can't have you work with me. Absolutely not. I won't be babied, and you'd only put your gigantic feet all over everything anyway."

Curtis took a second to interpret that and felt the slow dawn of joy. "Fine."

"And this isn't my fault. If you want to make a mull of your damn fool life, I can't stop you."

"No." Now Curtis couldn't stop grinning. "Are you always this difficult?"

"Yes."

"Are you ever going to make things simple for me?"

"I doubt it."

Curtis put out a gentle finger and tipped Daniel's chin up so their eyes met. "May I kiss you?"

"You just did."

"Yes. May I?"

"Oh, good *God*." Daniel grabbed a handful of Curtis's hair, pulling his head down so that their lips met in urgent collision. Curtis grunted, wrapping the slighter man in his arms, feeling Daniel sway forward at the exercise of his strength. He pulled tighter, and felt a gasp, then he was thinking of nothing but kissing Daniel, his tongue in the other man's mouth, feeling his lips and teeth, hands all over the slim body. He devoured him with the desperation that he hadn't let himself face until now, the need for Daniel in his arms that had been a burning urgency for days, until he felt Daniel gasping and trying to say something and reluctantly released his mouth.

He was leaning against a chest of drawers, he realised. Daniel was sitting on it with his legs wrapped round Curtis's hips, arms round his chest. He wasn't entirely sure how that had happened.

Daniel tilted his head back to look into Curtis's eyes. "Let the record show, I did try to put you off. And I'm not asking you for promises, or giving any."

"I don't expect you to, you awkward sod."

"Quiet. I truly hoped you wouldn't come here." He leaned forward again, resting his head against Curtis's chest, and whispered, "I dreamed that you would."

Curtis stroked his hair. "It's not the first time I've come after you."

Daniel's head was heavy against his ribs. "Oh, God, Archie. My Viking. You do not know how you have plundered me."

"You've such a turn of phrase," Curtis said hoarsely. "How could anyone not love your mouth."

Daniel gave a little choke of laughter. "You do go your own way, don't you?"

"So do you." He kissed the tousled black hair. "I wouldn't ask you to do otherwise."

Daniel's arms tightened. "This does not mean I'm going to put you at risk. We're going to be careful, hmm? I'm not turning your life upside down."

"You did that when you shook my hand and made a filthy remark about soldiers."

"*Suggestive.* It was suggestive."

"From you, it was filthy."

Daniel grinned unrepentantly. "If we're on the subject..." He reached up to brush his hand through Curtis's hair. "I never knew the most arousing sight in the world was a big man reading poetry. I could have watched you for hours. I could have gone to my knees for you there and then."

Curtis swallowed. Daniel's smile was wicked now. "On which note...have you missed me?" He slid his hands down to Curtis's waistband. Curtis moved his own hands to trap them.

"Just a moment. Will you work with me? Please?" He didn't say, *Will you let me protect you?*, though the words were pounding in his mind.

Daniel grimaced. "Do you want to work for your uncle? Truly?"

"I want to work with you." He leaned down to kiss the top of Daniel's ear. "Say yes."

"On a trial basis. No obligations."

"Of course." Curtis fought to keep back the smile that threatened to split his face.

"And no more barging into alarms. My nerves won't take it."

"Sorry."

"And if we find ourselves in that situation again, next time you're sucking *me* off."

"Fair enough. Do we have to wait until then?"

"Well, I suppose you do need the practice." Daniel's lips curved in that secret smile, and this time, at last, Curtis knew that he was in on the joke. "Watch and learn, my dear." He pushed Curtis gently back, for space, and slid elegantly to his knees. "Watch and learn."

About the Author

KJ Charles lives in London with husband, kids and cat. She is an editor by profession and writer by inclination and blogs about writing, editing, reading and book life. Find her blog and website at kjcharleswriter.com or follow her on Twitter @kj_charles.

It's all about the story...

Romance

HORROR

www.samhainpublishing.com

CPSIA information can be obtained at www.ICGtesting.com
Printed in the USA
LVOW11s0039051215

465433LV00005B/676/P